MR. DARK & SCARY

R.K. LATCH

D & T
PUBLISHING

To Kreature, for being a better daughter than I could ever deserve. I love you.

WINCHESTER COUNTY, MISSISSIPPI

APRIL

1

DEMONS SCREAMED ALL AROUND HER. Piercing wails stabbed at her eardrums.

Florence Webb shut her eyes and concentrated.

She pushed it. She pushed it all. Put her shoulder to everything all at once and shoved it as far as she could out of her mind.

After a moment, she could think again. Finally, she could hear her own voice in her head, a little less familiar than she'd have liked, but she could hear it.

Thankfully, Florence idled off the road before her little episode came on. She felt them sometimes before they attacked. Sometimes, not all. Her body was no longer hers. It belonged to the smack, and she would shrivel up and die without it.

It took several long minutes for her to regain control. Then, going through a routine of mental exercises she'd perfected herself, her heartbeat slowed, and she could breathe again.

Slowly, she pulled her father's Pontiac Chieftain back onto the road. Night had fallen, and there was little to no traffic to share the road with. Magnolia Lane was a small thin ribbon of a road that ran from the highway to the small community surrounding Tucker Lake. It was half-past nine, and everything except the one convenience store that doubled as a bait and tackle shop was closed up and dark inside.

Good. Florence didn't want to pass anyone she knew. Which, in all reality, wasn't likely. She didn't associate with the types of people that kept homes up at the lake.

At one time, she thought that would change, but sadly, that, like everything else in her life, had turned from sugar to shit.

The radio played low, but she wasn't listening to Dean Martin croon. It took all her focus to keep the car between the ditches. She had the shakes and couldn't keep her trembling hands still on the wheel for her life.

Florence passed through the tiny business section and onto Crescent Moon Lane, the road that encircled the lake and led to most of the homes.

Large, luxurious houses ringed the waterfront. Homes that probably cost more than her parents had made in their lives.

Too soon, she reached the familiar gate. The gate was closed tight. Florence eased into the driveway, butting the front of the car right up to the gate. She killed the headlights and the engine Shifting into reverse with one foot on the brake, she engaged the old car's parking pawl after killing the engine. It would be a long stroll up to the house from here, with no key for the gate.

She didn't step out of the car when she pushed open her door. Instead, she sat there a moment, collecting her thoughts. She'd played this out in her mind countless times over the last few days. But, now that the time was here, it felt like an impossible task.

Florence Webb was a once-promising young woman who'd reached her twenty-fourth birthday just one month ago. March 17, to be exact. Saint Patrick's Day. Florence didn't have an ounce of Irish blood in her (neither did she have Italian, a question one might have when asking how she got her unique name), but that was ok. In her humble opinion, Florence Webb had been lucky for most of her life. Life had been good. In her youth, she'd been a happy child. That had carried well into her early 20's.

Then she met what she thought was her Prince Charming,

Charles Renault, and everything changed. Not all at first, but slowly. Like a frog set down into a pot of lukewarm water on a stovetop. As the temperature rises, the frog doesn't realize it until it's too late, and he's boiled alive.

Older than her by two decades, Renault was a big man in her hometown of Farmington, Mississippi. He had a lot of pull and influence, and everyone knew and respected him. That had been attractive to young Florence.

Charles had noticed her at the diner where she worked. He started striking up short conversations when the place was slow, and soon Florence began looking more and more forward to his ever-increasing visits.

Then one night, Max Trund, who'd promised her a ride home she was actually looking forward to, didn't show.

Charles had wandered out after she'd waited almost a quarter of an hour. He offered her a ride home, but that's not where they went. Instead, they paid a visit to a Howard Johnson Motor Lodge an hour away.

Florence was swept off her feet. Being with the older, sophisticated Charles (always Charles, never Chuck or Charlie) wove a spell over Florence that she now feared she'd never break. But what had started as a wild love story straight out of a romance novel was now a sad state of affairs.

Now, here in this place, she knew she wasn't welcome. But she also had to admit that the lake was quite a sight this time of year. The bee's knees Florence had called it upon her first visit with Charles.

White tendrils of mist rose from the lake's placid surface. The county's smallest of two large lakes, Tucker Lake, was much more exclusive and secluded than Magnolia Lake. While both were quite picturesque, most of the land around Tucker was owned privately, while at Magnolia, the county-owned and operated much of the real estate. With that being the case, the property value at Tucker was much higher, and only those in the proper tax bracket could afford a lot, much less build the type of house that would fit in amongst the others.

The house was well-lit and private on two acres in front of her. It was the most prominent house down here at Tucker Lake. It was the summer house to beat all summer houses.

"You can do this. You have to do this."

She rubbed her stomach. Something moved in there that brought on a fresh wave of nausea.

The house was fancy, much fancier than Florence's parents' place, where she still lived. How long would they allow her to do that? The question became clearer every time she looked into their faces. Not much longer. They were a far cry from the folks that raised her.

No, that wasn't fair. She was lying to herself. It was her who changed. Not them.

She stood there on the dark porch for a time. She wasn't sure how long. Once she announced her arrival, things would go quickly. She knew her lover was here. There were more than the minimum lights ablaze inside. His car was in the drive, the hood still warm. She knew about such things from her father doing her the same way during her teenage years.

Finally, she committed.

Her knuckles rapping on the door echoed loudly across the silent lawn. Silence from inside the house. Nothing moved. She knocked again. And again.

Footsteps from the other side of the door. Low and distant but growing louder.

Charles yanked the door open with enough force to startle Florence even though she was standing there expecting it. As his eyes washed across Florence, his nostrils flared, his eyelids closed to slits, and a redness grew across his face.

"What in the fuck are you doing here, Barbie?" Her name was not Barbie, and it was no pet name he'd given her when they'd been going hard and heavy. Instead, it was a jab at her for the pills, the pills he got her hooked on in the first place. The pills he supplied. "I told you not to come around here. Cut out!"

Again, she expected his ferocity, but that did not help her handle it.

Then he took her in and really gave her a once over. He looked at her in the pale light that slipped past his tall form in the doorway.

Florence knew what he was seeing, and it broke her heart for him to see her in such a pitiful condition.

She'd seen herself. It was impossible to go all day long without confronting a mirror, the random baleful reflection in glass, or some other shiny surface. Florence looked like hell. Worse, really. Her hair hadn't been washed in weeks. It was greasy and foul and clung to her skin and clothes. Her once-tanned face was now the pale pallor of a corpse. She was thin. Much too thin. Her clothing draped over her more than she wore it. Her hips were sharp, and her ribs were pronounced.

Mere weeks. That's the time it had taken for heartache and physical addiction to pervert her youthful beauty.

Florence was no rock. She was not an immovable object. And she began to sob.

"I…I just needed to see you," she said through tears.

"Ok, you've seen me. And you look like shit, by the way. You can leave."

"No, Charles. I can't. I need to talk to you."

Charles rushed out onto the front porch. Grabbing her by each bicep in a tight, pinching embrace. "Listen here, little girl. We are through. We are finished. We are over. I never want to see your face again."

"I'm pregnant," she said before she even realized it.

Her words must've had unintended power because they caused a change in Charles Renault. If he'd been angry before, he was now a raging bull. A look came over his face that instantly froze Florence's blood. She'd seen it before, but only once, and it had been absolutely awful.

When he spun her and threw her roughly against the side of the house, she knew she'd messed up and was in for a repeat of that awful night.

As her back slammed against the wall siding, the air rushed from her lungs. An involuntary yelp escaped her.

"Why the fuck would you tell me that?" he demanded. She was flabbergasted. "It's not mine. No telling who the father is." His words hurt. They hurt more than being slammed into the wall. And he gave her no time to recover.

There was a firm hand around her throat. Then a second. She couldn't breathe. Charles was a strong man. That had been part of his allure. Though he was a businessman, he was in tip-top shape and more than a match for the decimated twenty-four-year-old woman. She was nothing more than a rag doll to him.

Her lungs burned like fire. She struggled against him, but it was of little use. Floaters, huge black dots, formed in her vision. Florence was fading from consciousness, and there wasn't a thing she could do about it. Charles' face was contorted from his effort.

Her sight faded to black. She struck out.

"Ugh," Charles grunted as his hot breath showered her face. His hands relaxed, and she broke free from his grip. He grabbed his groin and hobbled back. His cheeks burned brighter, and Florence moved back away from him. She knew a knee to the groin could be considered a cheap shot, but she didn't give one hot damn under the circumstances.

"Stupid cunt," Charles growled. He swung his arm in her direction, but she was just out of his reach, doing nothing but raking thin air.

"Charles, please, calm down. I didn't want it to be like this." He was hobbling toward her, already shaking off the pain of her well-placed attack. She really had no idea he would flip his lid like this.

She never saw the punch coming. She was looking him in the eyes, trying to find an ounce of compassion, maybe even love. There was none to be found. His knuckles connected with her stomach.

Florence stumbled back, throwing her arms up in defense, but he threw another wild haymaker, and this time, she was completely knocked off the porch. It was like being hit with the fist of God himself. Everything in her skull shook, her teeth trembled in her gums, and her eyes almost popped from their sockets.

She cleared the steps and landed on the damp grass face first. Hard. Her head hurt like hell, but something else was worse. There was severe pain growing in her abdomen.

"Charles, darling, what's going on?" A voice at the door. Florence turned her head to look but could see a silhouette crowned by the foyer light.

"Nothing. Absolutely nothing," Charles said. His voice was calming, and his breathing was returning to normal. "This young girl was just leaving, isn't that right, Barbie?"

Florence didn't—couldn't—say anything. Her pelvis was cramping uncontrollably, and all she could do was sob. Then, finally, she heard the door slam, and after a few minutes, she got to her feet, wiped the tears from her face and slowly, painfully made her way back to the car.

2

THE SUN WAS RISING JUST above the horizon. There wasn't so much as a single cloud overhead in the light blue sky. The world was still muted, still half-asleep. Mark Borden crossed the street from the sidewalk to the deep green grass of the courthouse lawn. Mark was a tall, lanky fella in his mid-forties. Dressed in dark blue coveralls and work boots, he was sweating as he walked briskly.

He usually bicycled to work, but he'd discovered a flat tire on his bike this morning and was high-stepping it so as not to be late. Having held the same job for over fifteen years, Mark took more than a bit of pride as the county courthouse's only custodian. As a result, he was rarely late and stayed over to finish his tasks when needed.

Mark was not the sharpest tool in the shed. And he knew it. He also knew that other folks wouldn't even be kind enough to consider him even a dull tool. So, he didn't let their opinion bother him. At least not often. His ma had been clear. If God didn't want him the way he was, he would have made him different.

Mark wasn't about to argue with God. His mother had even named him after the Mark in the Bible. He was called something more, but it was a big word. Mark never was good with big words.

But he remembered a lot of the smaller ones. Mark, with the big word, had been a very good man, his mother had told him. And he had to be good too, she had always told him. Even when other people weren't.

Surprisingly, that wasn't a significant issue in Mark's life. Folks treated him well enough. He kept to himself and didn't try to start many conversations. On the other hand, he had an awful stutter when he was nervous, and when he was around folks, he was always nervous.

But he didn't want to be late, just because he'd had a flat tire. It wasn't the county's fault. It was his problem, and he had to deal with it. Moreover, it would be wrong to delay his duties, and he might "get a talking to" from Mrs. Bonnie, an awful thing of an old woman if Mark had ever known one. While no one else ever seemed to have a problem with Mark's work, Mrs. Bonnie could always be counted on for a quick "You missed some dust bunnies down on the east hall" or "Someone's made a mess in the toilet, and it's been sitting there waiting on you all morning" to sour the mood.

Who knew? It might even be worse than a "talking to." While she wouldn't be in for hours, it seemed she always knew what Mark was up to, whether she was at work or not. He didn't overthink it. Or tried not to. It kind of spooked him.

He also knew that if he lost his job, he would have difficulty finding new employment. Times were hard across the South, including the little town of Farmington, and jobs were few and far between.

With no family left, not much in the way of savings, and no wife or girlfriend to help, Mark was entirely on his own. His salary from the county was modest, leaving little left over for luxuries and creature comforts. However, it paid his bills and allowed him to buy groceries and a few select items down at the Five and Dime, which would include a tube for his bicycle this time.

Mark stopped short on the far edge of the courthouse. Large Magnolia and weeping willow trees provided a little shade in the summer on all four sides, though neither was as shady as a lovely oak or maple over wooden benches. Four benches had been placed on the east and west sides of the building, where the grounds ran deep and wide. Only two were on the north and south, where the lawn was shallower. Mark had passed onto the south side, as the sun was just then brimming at the horizon with incredibly bright rays. Finally, on the nearest of the two benches, someone sat.

It was, of course, not unusual to be sitting on a bench in the shade of the trees and the three-story courthouse. But it *was* unusual this time of the morning, and he could tell, upon first glance, something wasn't quite copacetic here. Copacetic was a big word. He could remember that one. He liked that one. But he didn't like the feeling that fell over him by chancing upon the bench sitter.

Mark assumed the early morning visitor was female by the long hair draped over the back of the bench and the slight frame facing the big building.

He looked around. No one else in sight.

Then he noticed she was holding one hand up to the sky as if bathing it with the morning's light. Perhaps she was merely stretching after an extended sit. But that was her only movement, and while he could not know how long her arm had reached for the heavens, he knew she was not pulling it back to her.

It struck Mark how a kid in a classroom might raise their hand to ask the teacher a question. Mark had attended a few years of grammar school before his mother withdrew him. So, he knew what he was talking about.

It was a thin arm, but not delicate, muscled. Mark also saw the way the hand trembled.

Mark didn't want to startle the person. He didn't figure he was anyone's idea of handsome, but neither was he grotesque. Yet, he did seem to spook people through his lumbering appearance and his soft footedness more than he liked. So, he continued on from the side but took long strides with his left leg to bring him more and more into her periphery.

Mark halted a dozen feet from her and cleared his throat. The sound was noticeable but not abrasive.

The head didn't turn, the body didn't tense, and the hand remained aloft.

"Excuse me, ma'am," Mark said as gently as he could, still making sure his voice would carry. Nothing. No response.

This was proving stranger and stranger. He didn't want to be rude and continued to the double doors at the head of giant concrete steps a few dozen yards beyond her. This was proving to be one heck of a morning for Mark. First, the tire. Now, this. It was going to be one of those days, he was afraid.

He decided to try again. "My name is—" he could not get the rest out. The head turned to him abruptly, and suddenly he was staring at the saddest set of eyes Mark had ever had the misfortune to meet. They were even sadder than his ma's as she lay there dying, knowing she was leaving Mark alone to fend for himself.

They were the eyes of a young woman. Her chestnut brown hair, which grew past her shoulders, was matted and disheveled. A crust of something dark blue lay across her upper lips and even smeared her cheeks. She'd been wearing some kind of makeup around her eyes, smeared down her cheeks in great rivers of black. Mark didn't know much about that stuff; his ma had never worn it.

Mark did not know this woman's name, but he had seen her face. Many times. Farmington was a small place, and it didn't get a lot of out-of-towners. She might have been pretty, another place, another time. But, right here, right now, she looked like, well, she looked like hell.

Her bottom lip trembled. She closed her eyes and swallowed. Mark felt relief as their gaze broke. When her eyelids parted, Mark avoided them.

"Dead. It's dead," she said in a hoarse whisper.

Her hand fell from the sky. The movement was quick and sudden, and Mark took a step back on pure reflex. The next thing he knew, she raised a big, mean revolver from her lap that caught the new day's light and sparkled like glass.

"No, no," Mark heard himself say as realization hit him. He reached out for the woman's shoulder. Only inches away.

The tips of his long finger grazed her, digging trenches across the fabric of her pale-yellow blouse as she placed the gun's muzzle between her lips. He saw as she pushed it gingerly across her teeth and nudged it to a stop against the roof of her mouth. Then, with the thumb of her right hand, she squeezed the trigger. All of this was in agonizingly slow motion in which Mark could do nothing.

Never in all his years had Mark seen, much less felt, such an explosion. One second, the young woman's head was there, a whole thing. And the next, he could see clear through a gaping hole at the back of her head. Bits of bone, skull, cartilage, grey matter, flesh, and blood showered up like a burst pipe.

The gunshot boom was like rolling thunder in Mark's chest; for some reason, he felt a shock of electricity surge from his fingertips, shooting up his arm and sizzling throughout his body. Birds cried out and took flight from their perches in the trees.

Mark Borden stumbled backward, making a great effort to keep his footing. The world was different now. For a moment, he could hear nothing, see nothing. He wiped at his face and slung away the remains of the young woman's face.

Then the world was back, right there in front of him.

Too bright, too loud. The gentle breeze rustling the nearby Magnolia leaves sounded like bone grating against bone.

The body jerked upon the bench and then fell back against it, slumping as it settled.

"No, no, no, no, no, no," Mark chanted without even realizing it. He was still moving. Farther and farther away from the catastrophe. His legs had a mind of their own.

The step down from the courthouse to the lawn was a mere six inches, but it was enough to knock Mark off balance, and he fell backward.

A car horn blared. There was the high-pitched bark of rubber on asphalt. Mark turned to see the source of the noise, and the front end of a Studebaker crashed into him.

Mark Borden knew nothing else.

3

TWO WEEKS LATER...

THE VOICES BLEEDING through the walls were angry and cruel.

Yates Blevins lay in his bed with covers pulled tight over his head. His eyes were closed, and he was doing his absolute best to block out the sounds that he knew all too well.

His father was really on one tonight. Not that that was out of the ordinary. But tonight had been particularly bad. With his left hand, he held his right elbow tightly. The pain was intense. And if the horrible fiasco in the living room weren't enough, he would have to live with a broken arm for the next several months.

There would be no doctor's visit. There would be no cast. It was not his first broken bone, and Yates knew it would hardly be his last. That didn't make the pain any easier to bear, of course. Nothing would do that. But that hollering through the thin walls was taking his mind off it. At least for the moment.

"I'm sick of this shit, woman. God damn it. I work my fingers to the bone every day, and what do I come home to? A smart-mouthed woman and a sniveling kid," Roger Blevins shouted.

Yates strained his ears but could only hear a muffled murmur coming from his mother. He wanted nothing more than to throw back the blankets and jump from the bed, run from the room, knock his father against the wall with a staggering right hook, and kick him until he packed his things and left forever. But at nine years old and weighing less than a third of his father's body weight, with a broken right arm, that wasn't going to happen. He had his chance to fight back just earlier tonight, and like always, he'd acted the part of a coward.

It wasn't really his fault. Roger Blevins was a huge, strapping man, a real greaser, and as mean as any pissed-off rattlesnake had any right to be. Yates didn't have a chance against him, and both he and his father knew that.

Maybe his mother would do something, Yates thought as it happened.

He'd been playing with his toys on the living room floor. He was a lone gunman saving a beautiful damsel from bloodthirsty Indians. That was his routine most evenings when supper was finished while his mother cleared the table and washed the dishes.

And like most evenings, Yates' pa didn't darken the doorway of their home until well after the supper dishes had been cleaned and put away, and both he and his mother were preparing for bed.

Roger's shift at the old shirt factory didn't last that long. Yates didn't know where his father went every night, but he did know that some nights, he had the stench of beer and stale cigarette smoke. And on other nights, he smelled like whiskey. Those were the worst nights. Those were nights Roger, angry beyond reason, tormented Yates and his mother endlessly.

Tonight, it had been a broken arm—Yates was pretty sure it was broken, as he had experience in such matters. Before, it had been a wrist, his nose, blackened eyes, bruised and cracked ribs, the list going on and on. And with Roger not allowing the boy to see a doctor, should blame fall on him, Yates was left to heal the best he could.

His mother's scream broke him from his thoughts, and Yates pulled his covers tighter around him. A wall shuddered, and the house fell silent, but only for a moment. The quiet was soon pushed back by his father's gruff voice barking.

"Stop it, Roger, please," his mother called. The sound of her pleading caused his heart to ache. He would act as if he were just a little older if he were just a little stronger. But he was not Captain Marvel. Hell, he wasn't even a fully grown man.

He'd tried before to intervene, thinking himself a hero. But he'd learned real fast the brutal reality of being weak, helpless and defenseless. Even his mother admonished him for his attempt.

So, he lay there, terrified of his father's voice, hoping that he lingered with his mother and forgot all about him. So selfish, he knew, but he could not help himself.

Yates waited and tried his best to block out the sounds. Finally, the house fell quiet after a while and remained that way.

Peeking out from underneath his bedding, Yates saw it was almost midnight by his bedside alarm clock. The old man had most likely passed out on the sofa in front of the television. That's where he usually slept once his rampage died out. He would be up and gone before Yates would be up for school, which was some relief.

But not enough. His right arm was still swelling and would soon be twice its normal size. He was right-handed, too. His father knew that. He could no longer find a way to lay that was comfortable or even tolerable. Maybe if he could sneak into the kitchen, past his old man and grab some aspirin, they'd bring some slight relief. Yates pushed his covers off and was about to ease out of bed when he saw something in his bedroom window that struck fear into his heart.

Yellow eyes, bright in the darkness, shone in on him.

Yates Blevins was a young man who had known fear since being alive. Either at the hands of his father or the bullies at school. But never in his life had he felt the sensation that overtook him as he peered at those eerie golden orbs staring back at him. They were the eyes of a predator, like a panther or something else even more grisly.

Yates lay there, his blanket tossed aside. It was as if the eyes hypnotized him into stagnation.

The eyes came closer.

A face stared through the window at 9-year-old Yates Blevins, who was neither smiling nor frowning. Instead, it was a pale face, that of an older man, probably around the same age as Roger, Yates' father. It was a thin face, draped half in the nighttime and half-lit by the security light outside their little house. A long, pointed nose, deep-set, beady eyes and hair slicked back from a forehead covered in a scar. The disfigurement ran three inches long and a quarter-inch wide from the outside corner of his right eye in a diagonal line up into the hairline above the temple. The flesh was bright pink and puckered within the shallow wound.

It was a disturbing thing, indeed. Such a thing would catch anyone by surprise.

The icy fingers of fear wrapped themselves around his heart for a moment. Then, it passed. The man did not attempt to open the window, call him to the window, or do anything.

Instead, Yates finally saw the emotion on the man's face. The face fell as if seeing something disappointing, and at first, Yates was sure that was what the man was attempting to convey. But no, the way the eyes turned up, looking almost skyward, it was compassion or perhaps pity. But at that moment, Yates knew he had nothing to fear from the man.

The young boy watched the man bring his index finger up vertically to his lips, making the universal *shhh* gesture.

Yates nodded his agreement to keep quiet, and the man waved and stepped away from the window, the rusted-out Corvair up on blocks in the backyard now filling his view.

ROGER WAS A LITTLE OVER A SIX-PACK DEEP INTO A STUPOR AS HE SAT in front of the television with his eyes half-closed. He'd shed his work shirt and sat in his stained white undershirt and work pants. It was hot in the house, and a cloud of cigarette smoke floated due to the lack of air circulation. The fan was a meager thing that he could barely feel on his arms, much less his face.

The Zenith set was a luxury, one he could scarcely afford.

Nevertheless, it made tolerable the stifling heat and the stink of the Matchsticks, the overpopulated housing development the city and county had built for those less fortunate. Cheap lumber and cheaper hardware, nothing but matchstick houses. Ready to ignite with the first fiery spark.

But Roger Blevins worked hard five days a week, from sunup to sundown. And all he had to show for it was this shitty house, that nagging bitch wife of his and that sniveling little snot that Roger swore belonged to either a former mailman or milkman. Surely to God, his seed hadn't produced that little wimp.

If it had, his stock must've been sabotaged by something in Aubrey's family tree.

So yeah, he figured he deserved the Zenith.

The way he felt, he wouldn't make it to the bedroom. He rarely did. Instead, he often fell asleep on the couch in front of the set. Aubrey slept in the bedroom, of course. Good riddance. Who could sleep with that old crow gabbing on about this or that?

The sofa was hell on his back, but it was closer to the pisser and the fridge, so he made do.

A commercial interrupted his program, and he closed his eyes to rest them for a moment.

Peck--Peck--Peck came the sound. Like something tapping on glass.

Almost like a finger tapping on a window.

Roger was seated with his socked feet propped up on the coffee table next to his ashtray. Roger listened closely. He heard nothing else.

He'd almost convinced himself he'd heard nothing but the kitchen faucet having a random series of drips and then running dry when the sound came again, this time at a faster pace. *Peck-Peck-Peck.*

Roger swallowed and sat up. He set his beer bottle on the table before him but inadvertently knocked several empties to the floor. He scared himself and bolted to his feet, looking around the room.

He saw nothing but peeling paint, cheap framed photos covered in dust, and even cheaper furniture. But there was nothing there that would make the tapping sound.

Roger decided he should take a piss while he was already standing. That saying, "You don't buy beer, you only rent it," proved true one-hundred percent of the time.

The bulb in the bathroom was too bright, and he squinted as he got down to business.

Wood creaked behind him, and he twirled, spraying the sink and wall with a weak urine stream.

There was nothing there. Just the house settling. Roger admonished himself. He was not only a fool but a damned fool. Maybe the brew was part of a bad batch. That happens. Last winter, Roger drank a few too many and had the most vivid dream of a raccoon munching on his brain that stayed with him much longer than he liked to admit.

Finished voiding his bladder, he zipped up and turned back to the door.

A face stared right back at him. Less than six inches away. Roger's mind started to scream in panic. His heart prepared to jump up its tempo two-fold, but there was no time. Before Roger could react, or even hope to decide to react, something hard hit him in the side of the head, and everything went dark.

4

LAMAR COLEMAN THOUGHT the steering on the old wrecker was loose as a one-dollar hooker, cursing the damn truck. Burney Walker, his boss man, should be ashamed of his cheap, stingy ass for making Lamar drive this piece of shit. But Lamar knew why he did it, or at least a good idea. Lamar was a negro, and old man Burner seemed to have a problem with dark-skinned folks.

He should have gone on home hours ago. It was well after dark, and dinner would be getting cold. But, of course, that assumed that no count slut he married had even bothered to cook tonight. You never could tell about her. Lamar worked for the last two years from sunup to sundown, and sometimes later, as tonight, to provide for his wife and his two young babies, and what thanks did he get? None, that's what kind.

The shop was dark as Lamar pulled up. He figured it would be. As usual, all the other folks were gone by quitting time. It was different for a tow truck driver. While Lamar worked an entire shift here in the junkyard through the day, he took calls on nights and weekends with the wrecker. It was much-needed extra money, but it didn't come easy. And it went too damn fast.

Lamar was still a young man, hardly twenty-four, but these long nights were still hard on him.

He was bringing in a fancy Plymouth, dead on the side of the highway. The owner had hiked several miles before getting a ride down to the truck stop to get to a phone. Some city fella in big city duds. Asked Lamar if the car could be repaired by midnight. It was all Lamar could do to not laugh in the fancy gentleman's face.

Lamar handed the man Burney's card and told him to call the shop after eight in the morning. The man didn't like it, but he was left with no other options. There wasn't an all-night garage around for a hundred miles. And the Plymouth wouldn't be making that trip.

Beyond the mechanical issues, the car was something to see. A real beauty. As Lamar lowered it from the rigging right up next to a shop wall, he admired how the pole lights danced across its shiny brightwork. The rear fins looked like they would slice through the air when up to speed.

As he finished up with the car, he kicked a bit of gravel with his booted toe. Some folks had more money than sense. A car like that would cost enough to turn his whole life around. No more dons in the mail. No more nagging wife. No more damned ankle biters keeping you up all hours of the night. If it was his car, he'd sell it as soon as possible, pack his bags, and be in the wind.

Gone forever from this life that had ground him down so.

But it wasn't his to sell, and he dared not even think about such things. Hell, they'd toss a negro like him in a cell beneath the jail and throw away the key.

A clatter inside the shop caused Lamar more than a bit of alarm. He stopped, looked around and reached into the back of his truck for a tire iron. He felt better as he gripped it tightly in a fist.

Burney lived up on the hill in a lovely brick house. The old man was as deaf as a post, so someone could rob the whole place under his nose if they had a mind to do so. Lamar had told him as much in the past, but Burney paid him no mind, as usual.

Another sound, this time of metal clanging against metal,

reached Lamar's ears, and he felt his heartbeat start to race. He grabbed the tire iron as if it were a baseball bat and stepped up to the plate. Burney wasn't paying him shit, but Lamar wasn't about to stand here and let the shop get ransacked.

Besides, he'd probably get blamed for it, knowing Burney. Lamar was a lot of things, but he wasn't a thief. And he was certainly no coward.

There were only two ways into the garage. The two twin roll-up doors at the eastern end and a personnel door set on the side. It was a big wooden building with tin for a roof instead of shingles and was loud as hell when it rained, not to mention hot during the summer and cold during the winter. Upon first glance, it looked as if nothing had been disturbed. But Lamar knew damn well something had to be making the noises he'd heard.

Burney kept a whole clowder of cats around, and they managed to get in and out of the shop even when closed up tight, but he doubted they were the cause of the commotion. Maybe something got in after them.

The man-sized door was unlocked and creaked slightly as he pushed it open. Inside, the shop was dim but not dark. Several of the overhead lights had been left on. That was unlike Burney. He was so tight-fisted with his money that he acted like he was on the brink of poverty instead of being more flush with cash than your average lawyer.

"Hello," Lamar called. When no answer greeted him, he felt silly.

The shop's interior held on to the day's heat; before he knew it, Lamar was sweating.

It was an automobile repair shop like any other. Well, not as well cared for or clean or stocked with the latest tools, but it was certainly not out of the ordinary. There were several vehicles in varying states of repair. Work lights still hung from their hoods, and while it was a rule for the grease monkeys to put away their tools daily, they were often left spread out around current projects. The floor was concrete, stained dark by oil and other fluids. Each step he took echoed.

An engine hung suspended from the ceiling on the sturdy chains of a hoist. The motor was still, the chains unmoving. Lamar didn't even want to think about what a mess it would make if it fell.

Lamar saw no cats, no other animals, no nothing.

"Fuck this," he said. "Nothing here that ain't supposed to be but me."

"Leaving so soon?" a hoarse voice whispered. Startled, Lamar spun, his eyes wide, the tire iron back up and at the ready.

"Who's there?" he called. No one answered. "Damn it, I said, who's there?"

Suddenly Lamar's surroundings didn't look so ordinary anymore. The shadows loomed larger. The light seemed to grow weaker. Lamar's hands worked up and down the tire iron, which now felt thin and unsubstantial.

At that exact moment, Lamar began thinking just how isolated Burney's shop was. Besides the old man at the top of the hill, there wasn't anyone around for at least a few miles. Long miles at that. And Burney himself would be about as much use as tits on a boar hog.

Lamar was as brave as any man he knew. Yet, standing there in the shop, he felt small, insignificant, and vulnerable. Those emotions were not foreign to him, not at all. He knew them from before. When he was just that. But that had been long ago, many years back. But that sickening sting they delivered was still familiar after so much time.

"The fuck is here? Show yourself, you scared little bitch."

"Oh, now. I'm no bitch." The voice seemed to issue from nothing but a deep dark shadow. Lamar peered closer, but the darkness only appeared deeper, more profound than possible. The voice was barely more than a hoarse whisper but impossible to miss. It chilled Lamar down to his very marrow.

"But if I were a dog, boy, you couldn't tame this hound." The voice and the shadows seemed to be mocking him now. The shadows crept steadily outward, consuming the interior of the auto repair shop. Then he saw them. Twin orbs of such a hateful yellow,

Lamar's first instinct was to look away. But instead, Lamar blinked, unable to believe his eyes. It was as if the darkness was moving.

"Fuck this," Lamar said and turned to flee. It was then that strong hands grabbed him from out of nowhere. He was lifted from his feet. And not gently, and then just as the ceiling was rushing toward him, there was a sickening halt, and he was slammed down onto the concrete.

His head smacked hard against the floor, instantly cracking his skull. Pain blossomed out through every extremity. Above him, the monstrous big block Chevy motor rocked back and forth, once, then twice.

The hoist was an expensive one, all-electric and well-installed. However, when the release engaged, it became just a simple hoist, and the chains clattered like a hundred delicate dishes jangling in a cabinet during an earthquake.

The monstrous chunk of American engineering fell swiftly and decisively straight down. Squashed like a giant bug, Lamar Coleman's body exploded. Bits of bone, gore and blood showered the immediate area.

Then as if nothing at all happened, the shop was silent as a tomb once more.

5

"SOMETHING'S GOT to be done, gentlemen. The whole town is a powder keg about to blow," Mayor Beau Sandford said. He was a thin, tall man with grey hair cut into a flat top. He'd served as mayor of Farmington for four terms, and you could see by the look in his eyes that he was tired. Now, this was landing in his lap.

The mayor's office was located on the top floor of the Winchester County Courthouse. The county leased out some of its available space as the municipal offices were small in number and staff. It worked for the city by saving them the cost of building offices and helped the county with a steady influx of cash.

Sandford's office was nothing grand and furnished on the cheap, but it was spacious, and there was seating for everyone. Quite a group was assembled, to say the least. Besides the mayor, the sheriff, C.W. (Sparky) Sparkman, the district attorney, Willie Barnes, Cy Carpenter, the chairman of the board of aldermen, Jessie Green, the president of the board of county supervisors, Tom Harper, a state highway patrolman that lived just outside of town, and Mildred Doran herself, descendent of the county's founder and the first and only female county judge.

No one asked why Jeff Kathy, the publisher of the Daily Farmer, the only newspaper published for fifty miles, wasn't in attendance. His good-natured questions had turned pointed and brash soon enough, and no one here had any answers to print in the morning edition.

"People deserve answers," Cy Carpenter, a crotchety old geezer with a piss-poor attitude on the best of days, spat out.

"I agree," the mayor responded.

"With all due respect, Beau, we don't have any answers to give them. Hell, why are we pretending otherwise?" the district attorney provided.

"We know enough. Somebody is out there killing. Killing like he has a fucking—" Tom Harper stopped midsentence and nodded toward Judge Doran. She gave a hurried wave to continue. She had the mouth of a sailor, and they all well knew it, but manners were something hardwired in. "...taste for it. We can tell them that. Let everybody know what it is we're facing."

"But who is doing the killing? Who is mutilating their own fellow citizens? Is it man, or is it something else?" Jessie Green asked. It was the question they'd all, even Sandford, had not wanted to be the one to ask. They all looked to the judge.

"How the hell should I know, fellas?" She was a tall woman, now going gray but still possessing grace only afforded the truly regal. She was rough and gruff but could charm any man or stare one down just as easily. "The Winchester blood didn't come with any kind of instruction pamphlet. So I'm as clueless as anyone else here. Well, not as clueless as Sandford, but who the hell is?" It was a good-natured rib, and despite the poor timing, it seemed to help them collectively reach a decision.

The Winchester family was as storied as it was reclusive these days. Having founded the county in the middle of the last century, the Winchester family began a drastic ascent into prosperity, power and tragedy. It was a name that was not only respected far and wide but also revered in some circles. While the family line was mostly watered down, and there were very few living descendants, those still around enjoyed the old family money and reputation. Mildred

Doran served unofficially as the town matriarch and her official duties.

The mayor was turned in his chair. He looked out the window overlooking downtown. Jesus, he loved this place. Always had. It had been the safest place he knew, despite some rather sinister peculiarities. Spring was here in full swing. The magnolia trees lining the street were in lush excellence, and the bushes were sprouting their greenery for spring. It was a shame that the season had brought not only blooms and blossoms but also blood.

Farmington was home, and now something evil had come to his home once more. But was he the man he used to be? Should he have stepped down in the last election? Probably. But he hadn't. So this was still his town and, therefore, his fight.

"You're right, Cy. You're all right. These awful murders must stop. Besides, folks are talking anyway. Hell, they're down to panic. So we can at least set the record straight, as far as we know it. Are we on the same page with the details? People will come to us individually, I'm sure. We have to keep our stories straight. Make sure we are all on the same page."

The sheriff wasn't sure everyone was the way they all looked around, like not wanting to be the pupil the teacher called on. So he recited what facts they had: "Three murders in less than two weeks. The first one was last Tuesday, April 9."

"About a week after that poor girl—," Barnes said but was cut off by Sparkman.

"Yes, six days."

"The first victim was Roger Blevins. At least that we know about. Happened on his property out in the Matchsticks. We're convinced he was moved from the house to the toolshed. Then, while he was attached to a workbench, someone broke every major bone in his body, dislocated joints, and, we are fairly certain with Dr. Walsh's assistance, he had his carotid artery severed by a blade. Took his family a full day to find him."

"Second, Lamar Coleman, the guy that drove the wrecker for Burney. Burney walked in one morning and found old Lamar, a big

Chevy block sitting on him. Burney said Lamar had brought in a tow the night before. Brought it back and parked it. Who knows what happened after that."

"That was the black guy who married that woman from out of state and moved out by your daddy's house, wasn't it, Sparky?" Jessie asked.

"Yep. Pop said he seemed a decent enough fella."

"Could have been an accident," the judge said, unwilling to go off on that tangent.

"Maybe, but what business did he have inside, screwing around with an engine hoist," Sparkman responded.

"Gentlemen, back to the matter at hand. We aren't investigating at the moment. But, as it were, we're getting our ducks in a row," Mayor Sandford said.

"Yeah," they both agreed.

"Go ahead, Sparky," the mayor said.

"The third apparent homicide was Harry Watts. Worked over at the utility department. The young man was not even married a full year yet. Played football up at the high school last year. Found out in his truck, with the truck still running about 6 a.m. His wife thought he hadn't come home, but he apparently drove home and was… disemboweled…inside the cab of his Chevrolet. Amanda, his wife, found him when she woke to start breakfast and saw the truck and noticed the exhaust rising. The killer left nothing behind, not even a bloody handprint.

"So, best we figure," Sparkman went on. "All three homicides were committed overnight. The best we can get from the doctor is anywhere from 11 p.m. to about 4 a.m. We say it's a man. Not saying it's something else, but it could be a woman. It's just not likely. "

"According to who?" the judge asked.

"Statistics, ma'am. It's really all we have to go on right now." Doran nodded at his answer.

No one said a word as Cy Carpenter swallowed hard and loud enough for everyone in the room to hear him. If nothing else, they knew how he felt.

"Surely to goodness there has to be some good news," the mayor said.

No one said a word for a moment.

"Actually, there is something," the sheriff said. "The missing girls, you know, the ones from Lee, Alcorn, and a few others?" He looked around, and a few nodded. Some didn't. "Over the last few weeks, a rash of kids have gone missing. Young girls. Prepubescent, all of them. So far," the sheriff stopped and rapped his knuckles on the mayor's desk in a gesture of good luck, "we have had no reports of missing minors, boys or girls. Hopefully, it will stay that way."

"Killers, kidnappers, just what kind of world do we live in?" Willie Barnes said aloud.

"The only one we have," the mayor answered.

"Do we all have it?" the judge asked, looking like she'd rather be anywhere but here. Everyone agreed whether they did have it or not. It was the best to be expected. For the most part, politicians are feckless, no matter their political leanings or stances, but they are smart enough to follow along after someone else, keeping their necks off the chopping block. Even small-town players aren't immune, but by and large, there tends to be one or two in the mix that is made of sterner stuff. With this group, it was Sheriff Sparkman and Judge Doran. While neither actually answered to the mayor, they both let him think he was making the calls. Harper was an outsider, and Doran, well, was a woman. Best not to upset the status quo.

"All right, folks," the mayor started after clapping his hands together. "Here's what we'll do. Willie, you reached out to Kathy this afternoon, right after this. It's too late to put anything out today, but we'll catch tomorrow's edition. Sparky, you stop by at WBDI and see if Cletus is still around. If not, talk to Bobby. Tell them the truth, tell them—" the phone rang, cutting off the mayor.

It rang and rang. Whoever it was on the other end was adamant. Sandford picked up the receiver. "Yes?" He listened for a moment. They all tried to, but the conversation was all too brief. Finally, the mayor took the phone from his ear and handed it to Sparkman. "It's for you, sheriff," the older man said.

Dread hovered over them like an invisible storm cloud but no less potent for being unseen. Every single one of them felt it in their bones.

6

SHERIFF SPARKMAN PLACED the receiver back on the handset and took a deep breath. He tried to process what he'd just heard.

"Well," Cy asked. "Tell us."

"There's been another?" the judge rightly guessed.

"Yes," the sheriff said solemnly, addressing them all. "Another. One more human being murdered in cold blood."

"Who, who is it, Sparky?" Old Man Carpenter asked.

"Renault. Charles Renault." The mayor and the judge spoke the same profanity simultaneously, but no one noticed. This was going to escalate quickly now.

"The old man ain't gonna be quiet for this," Willie said.

"No, he won't, and he has enough money to make problems for all of us and do nothing to find the culprit," Jessie said.

Quickly, everyone finished wrapping up the "official" story, leaving out Renault for the time being. They would need to see the scene and see if they could piece anything together before Charles' father and the public received proof that the stories they were speculating about were closer to reality than they would want to imagine.

"Change of plans," the mayor said. "Sparky, looks like you're going to be busy. Jessie, you hit up the radio station." They all nodded.

"Good luck to you all, especially you, Sheriff," the mayor said, and they were dismissed. Everyone began slowly shuffling out of the office. Everyone except Sparkman. He sprinted out, not exactly in a panic, but close. It had been a rough two weeks for everyone, especially the sheriff. Harper decided to follow him to Renault's.

When everyone was gone, Sandford remained seated behind his desk. The silence in the now-empty office was welcome. Beau Sandford was turning seventy-two this year, and as much as he hated to admit it, not for the first time, he was getting too long in the tooth to manage a town like Farmington. Time was, he'd jumped up and hurried down the stairs right behind Sparky, if not leading the way.

That was a young man's world, and he was no longer fit for it.

There was a soft knock at the door. "Come in," the mayor called.

Mark Borden pushed open the door and rolled in his metal janitorial cart. The mayor looked up and smiled.

"Evening, Mark. How're things?"

"Uh, fine, sir. I hope I'm not bothering you."

"No, not at all. I've never been one to stand between a man and his duties." Mark smiled. The mayor noticed the bandage on his forehead. "How are you doing, Mark? That was a nasty accident the other week."

When the mayor spoke, Mark Borden had pulled a broom from the cart and swept at the baseboards. He stopped, instinctively raised a hand to the bandage and replied. "It was. About scared the ever-loving mess out of me."

"Son, you could have been hurt a lot worse."

Mark was a tall man, a bit over six feet tall but thin, and he walked hunkered over, reminding many of the courthouse staff of the hunchback of Notre Dame. His hair was a dirty blonde, long and greasy and in dire need of a cut and wash. Approaching his mid-forties, he was single, and his only living relative had been his mother, who passed away two years ago.

Beau was convinced the fella was slightly retarded, but he did good work and didn't get in anyone's business, so he was tolerated to a degree. No one would stop by his house for Thanksgiving dinner or invite him to a poker game. But no one had a problem letting him empty their trash or mop their floors.

"Yes, sir. Thank God for small favors."

"Indeed," the mayor said. "Working late, aren't you? Don't you quit about five?"

Mark nodded. "Yes, sir. But I was out a few days and need to catch up."

"I see, I see," the mayor said. He smiled and looked back to his desktop, shuffling some papers and straightening others. Mark returned to his work. The mayor tried to keep a neat and tidy office, but people were in and out all day long, and things got dropped, shoved around, dusty, and generally dirty.

Mark finished in a little under ten minutes. Beau was glad to have his office back in order.

Mark, always quiet, waved to Beau as he pushed his cart back out the door. Nice enough, guy, Beau thought.

But damn, hadn't the fellow almost died when he fell into the street and the Studebaker ran into him? He'd just been arriving at work, so it could have been quite a predicament if Mark pressed it, but either he didn't know the law well enough or had no interest in recouping his medical expenses. The bill probably hadn't even been sent out yet, to be honest.

And what the poor guy had witnessed making him run into the street gave Beau chills just thinking about it. Of course, the fact that Mark, who'd had a stutter as long as Beau had known him, suddenly could converse normally wasn't lost on the mayor, but neither did he dwell on it.

MARK DIDN'T DRIVE. HE'D LEARNED HOW BACK IN HIS TEENAGE DAYS, but keeping the maintenance up on an automobile was too expensive for his liking. For a week after his accident, he hadn't had the balance to ride his bike, and the walk to and from work was nice at first, but the fifteen-minute trip wasn't nearly as nice in the evenings after working all day.

Now that he was back on his bike with a new inner tube, he made it less than half the time and used less energy. Mark lived in the same house in which he'd been raised. He never knew his father. He only grew up hearing about him. His mother had often told him he'd been a great war hero in the first World War. His mother had raised her only child independently. She'd been a good, sweet woman, and Mark missed her dearly.

That was all the family he knew of. He wasn't sociable, and besides a few of the neighbors that lived around him for years, Mark didn't meet new people easily and tried, as hard as he could, to live his life in solitude and peace.

He'd been successful in doing so since his mother died until the day of the accident. But, then, the car had really rung his bell. And the girl, the girl on the bench.

His mind was occupied throughout the day, and he rarely relived that atrocious time. Evenings and nights were the hardest as he didn't have much to keep him busy.

Mark picked his bicycle up off the ground and hefted it up the front steps. They were wooden and felt spongy underfoot. He had no idea how to repair them but knew he'd have to do something before next summer. The house was small, simple, and unadorned.

The Borden home had been paid off for a generation before his grandmother passed, and Mark's mother, Gertrude, had done everything in her power to keep it. But, until Mark was old enough to work, times had been hard.

Keeping the house in good shape was a matter of pride for Mark. There was nothing easy about being a homeowner, but it sure beat the heck out of renting a room down at the boarding house. Here, he was reminded of his life before his mother went away.

All the framed photos still clung to the walls, and Mark was studious about dusting them twice a month. Her bedroom was almost like the day she left this world. Bed linen changes and freshening were also part of his routine.

Before changing out of his coveralls, Mark headed to the back porch and pulled a tarp off his manual push lawnmower. It was the kind with a cylinder of blades that rotated when pushed.

It took him almost an hour to finish cutting the grass. A few folks had walked down the sidewalk as he was working. He waved at each one, whether or not they waved first or even returned the greeting.

Finally, dripping with sweat, he pushed the mower back up onto the porch, stepped inside and pulled a glass bottle of Coca-Cola from the icebox. Then, instead of taking a seat at the kitchen table, he stepped back outside, the wire screen door smacking shut behind him.

Full summer wasn't here yet, but it wasn't too awful far away. Mark plopped down in one of two twin wooden rockers. The glass bottle was sweating. Fat drops of condensation dripped down on his pants, but Mark paid no mind. There wasn't much in life better than a cold Coke.

Mark sat there long after the day gave way to night. The streetlights buzzed on, and still, Mark sat. Finally, as it neared ten o'clock, he got up from his rocker and went inside.

There was no air conditioning in the house, but several fans in the windows created a crosswind that relieved the worst of the day's built-up heat.

After a cold shower and brushing his teeth, Mark finally walked into his bedroom. Though it had changed slightly over the decades, it mostly remained that of a young boy. Mark's mother had never seen much use in changing it, and neither had Mark after her passing.

Like the house, the bedroom had been one of Mark's few happy places. Or it had felt happy until recently.

He couldn't wait to get home when they'd released him from Winchester General after his accident. And that first night, everything had gone well. It was the morning after when things went sideways.

When he awoke, he was lying atop his blanket and sheets. Odd, as he never went to sleep that way, he was anything but a wild sleeper, often waking in the same position as he'd been the night before. Not that morning. And his sleeping state was just the beginning.

The shoes he'd been wearing, kicked off into a far corner, were covered with red dirt and a little mud. It was odd. He clearly remembered kicking them off the night before. They had been mudless, if not exactly clean.

And he barely recognized his own reflection in the bathroom mirror. Sure, he was excited and confused, but the face staring back at him wasn't. In fact, it looked cool, calm, collected, and even a bit sinister.

In fact, while Mark's face was undoubtedly the one looking back at him, it was as if he barely recognized it.

Nothing he'd ever experienced could compare to that alienation. Like he didn't belong in his own skin. It was something he hadn't been able to shake.

But that hadn't been the only time. Three more since that first morning. All as disconcerting if not as novel as the first time.

Mark Borden did not deal well with stress. And this mystery that had come over him in recent weeks was quite a stressor.

His stomach hurt more days than not. It was a deep, burning sensation. Mark wasn't much for doctors but would have to break down and see one if it didn't improve. But, at times, he was thankful for the pain. It kept his mind occupied.

Now, as he readied himself for bed, he was tired and cozy from the shower, but his sore stomach churned, and he felt apprehension heavy on his mind as he crawled beneath the sheets.

But almost as soon as his head hit the pillow, Mark Borden was asleep.

His hands twitched at the wrists when he sunk into steady, deepening sleep. A quick but complete flick, fingers splaying apart, back together, and a second twitch of the wrist coming back into a rest position.

Another quick twitch.

Finally, a third. And he was still.

Then something, someone else, woke in Mark's stead.

7

"I AM SO sick of your shit, Geraldine," Rocky Moss shouted. They were in the kitchen. The icebox door stood open, revealing empty shelves.

"Sweetheart, I'm sorry. I didn't have enough money to—"

"It's always the same thing with you. You didn't have the cash. Couldn't fit it into the budget. Blah, blah, blah. For crying out loud, what does a man have to do to get a goddamned beer after working all day long?"

Geraldine was smaller than her husband by a fair margin. He towered over her shorter frame at five feet, ten inches by almost a whole foot. Rocky also outweighed the tiny Geraldine and had no problem throwing his weight around.

"Rock, I had to pay bills." Geraldine was trying to appease her husband. But, after ten years together, she was well aware of his turbulent temper.

"If you had the sense God gave a rock, you could have figured something out. Hell, I give you plenty of money."

"Plenty of money?" she asked incredulously. "Rock, it doesn't go as far as you think. I have to buy groceries, pay bills and everything else. Trust me, it's not plenty of money."

"Your backtalk is really starting to get to me," Rocky said as he moved toward her and stared down, glowering.

Geraldine clammed up with him standing over her. She was no fool, or at least she told herself that. She could smell the beer on his breath, which was nothing new. Although, to be honest, she'd be surprised if she didn't smell alcohol on his breath.

He'd stopped by the bar on his way home, she knew. It was his routine and where most of the money he accused her of spending ended up. She didn't care, really. The more he was away from home, the better.

"What? Nothing sassy to say now?" he taunted.

Geraldine had been pretty once. Years ago.

She now looked old and fatigued, but she was barely thirty. Her simple dresses were mended by hand. She'd long ago given up makeup as Rocky considered it a luxury he would no longer pay for. He'd also accused her of dolling herself up to catch another man.

If he only knew. Geraldine would be fine if anything ever happened to him, never remarrying for all her days.

"Rock, please," she urged, "you'll wake up Danielle." He shoved her then, hard. Geraldine fell roughly against the wall, almost tripping over a dining room chair. A large decorative wooden spoon and fork set fell from the wall to the floor.

She stumbled forward from the wall, right back at him. He must've really run the old bar tab tonight because instead of merely sidestepping his wife of all these years, letting her fall to the floor, he did something he'd done only a handful of times in all their matrimony.

Geraldine was still bent slightly at the waist, her arms windmilling to the sides to keep her balance. Her face was just too good of a target for him to resist.

Rocky's hands curled into big, beefy fists, and he stepped out with his right leg, swinging his shoulder and belted her right in the side of the head. The impact made a ringing clapping sound that echoed off the kitchen walls.

Geraldine crumbled to the ground.

"Don't tell me what to do," Rocky said, pointing his finger at her. She hadn't been knocked out completely, but she was dazed.

Geraldine flinched, bringing her arms up to protect herself. But unfortunately, that did nothing but piss Rocky off more. He grabbed her by the arm and snatched her up off the floor.

"I'm so sick of even looking at you," Rocky said. Then, Rocky threw her right back down to the floor using his entire body weight. Geraldine landed and rolled over once, not even attempting to rise.

"Daddy?" a little girl spoke up as she walked barefoot into the kitchen. Geraldine was shocked to see Danielle awake and out of bed. But who could blame her? Her father was in here making enough noise to raise the dead.

Rocky turned from his wife. Danielle was a daddy's girl, but she often lay in her bed and cried when he got on a roll like this. Finally, Geraldine figured she must've thought her father was hurting her mother and decided to intercede. It sure wasn't the first time.

Good intentions, but a bad decision.

Little Danielle took small steps as she ran and wrapped her arms around Rocky's legs. "Please don't fight, Daddy. Don't fight with Momma."

Rocky said nothing to his daughter, but to Geraldine, he said, "Look what you've done, you stupid bitch. You've woken her."

"Nu-uh. You did, Daddy," Danielle said. But she was crying now. Rocky didn't seem to care. Instead, he kicked her off his legs. She fell back on her rump, and her cries notched higher. Geraldine reached for her.

"See, look at you both. Two fucking peas in a pod. I'm getting out of here. You two can sit there and cry all fucking night, but I don't have to be here to listen to it."

"Rocky, please..." Geraldine called, but Rocky was no longer listening.

Rocky turned, almost tripping over his own feet. Then, looking around the kitchen, he spotted his car keys. He scooped them up and pushed them out through the carport door. He didn't even take the time to look over his shoulder. For if he had, he'd have seen his daughter with her hands out, begging for him to stay.

Perhaps that would have saved him.

Rocky almost tripped again, coming out the door. However, he managed to keep his balance and made his way to the driver's side of his raggedy Plymouth. He flopped in behind the wheel. It took him a few tries to get the correct key into the ignition.

The car started after three attempts. He ran off the driveway once before getting backed out onto the road. Once there, he slipped the car into drive and eased on the accelerator. The old car coughed and bucked but began accelerating.

Rocky didn't adjust the radio. It was already tuned to a country and western station. A man like Rocky had no use for that godawful noise all the kids were listening to these days. Folks like Elvis Presley and Jerry Lee Lewis were just charlatans shaking their bodies on stage for the foolish girls and stupid dames. No musical talent whatsoever, in his opinion. Just hypnotizing the young girls in a wholly obscene manner.

"All right, big boy, turn that hound dog croonin' shit off," a man said from the back. The car swerved, and Rocky's heart skipped a beat.

His eyes darted up to the rearview, but something hard hit him in the side of the head.

But Christ, what he'd seen!

He almost shat himself then and there. He might have if his supper had been more substantial than Jack Daniels. But, instead, the sight of those ungodly eyes, the color of a sick man's urine, chilled him deep down inside, in places he didn't know could chill.

"Keep your eyes on the road, idiot," the voice from behind whispered loudly. It was hateful and cruel and all too harsh. It turned Rocky's inside to jelly almost as much as those awful orbs that felt like they bore into the back of his head.

"WHAT ARE YOU DOING IN MY CAR? WHAT THE HELL IS GOING ON?"
Again, another thump to the head.

"Quiet, Rocky. You're not dealing with your wife and kid now."
Rocky didn't like that, and his whole face turned red. But his head
still throbbed, so he didn't part his lips to say another word. "There
we go. Looks like we understand each other."

Rocky continued down the road, driving slowly and scanning
for other cars.

"Looks to me like you're maybe looking for a cop. Are you
Rocky?"

"No, of course not."

"Good. Because I have a very serious gun pointed at your back
through the seat. Make me nervous, I pull the trigger. Behave, and I
won't. We clear?"

"Yeah."

"What's that?" The stranger bashed him in the side of the head
once more. "I'm your fucking elder boy. Show some manners."

"Damn it," Rocky yelped as the blow struck him. "Okay, yes, sir,
mister, fella, whatever. Just stop hitting me."

"I don't really care for any of those," the voice whispered. It was
like acid dripped from his words. "I've been called many things. The
shadow in the darkness, the night wraith, but my personal favorite,
I would say, is Mr. Dark and Scary. Has a nice ring to it, don't you
think, Rocky?"

Rocky couldn't be entirely sure if the man was joking or not.
This whole encounter was bizarre. While there was nothing light-
hearted about his current situation, the man behind him seemed to
be in the embrace of slight levity. The only thing that made sense to
Rocky was the man wasn't all there in the head. A few bricks short
of a wall, that sort of thing.

"Uh, okay," he finally managed.

"Now, take a right up here at the stop."

"Where are you taking me?"

"That's for me to know and you to find out." The man chuckled.

Quick and strange and totally unexpected. His voice had been threatening and harsh. The chuckle, while not the joyful sound of a circus clown, seemed out of place.

Jesus Christ, Rocky thought, this fellow isn't just a few bricks short. He's completely off his rocker.

8

THE PLYMOUTH'S headlights sliced through the deepening dark. The car's suspension was shot, and the whole car creaked and groaned over every bump. And there were a lot of bumps.

Mr. Dark and Scary steered Rocky west, out into the farming country. The road unfurling in front of them went from paved to gravel and finally to dirt. Then, nothing but pitch black could be seen beyond the car's headlamps. Of course, there were fields of crops: soybean, corn and cotton. Farmhouses were scattered sporadically, and even a few ranches with full complements of livestock. But they might as well have been traversing the Sahara Desert for all they could see out the windows.

Dark wasn't interested in sightseeing, and from the foul ammonia odor permeating the car, Rocky needed to worry more about controlling his bladder than roadside diversions.

"Roll down a window if you can't hold your piss, you filthy fuck."

"I-I couldn't help it," Rocky said. He'd become whiny after being told a gun was on his back. Funny how that worked, Mr. Dark thought. He watched as Rocky used his left hand to crank down the window. Cool night air spilled into the car, taking away the worst of the piss stench.

"Slow down. We're almost there," Mr. Dark said.

"Where?" Rocky asked. He looked around, concerned.

"To where the hell we've been going, dimwit," the man admonished Rocky. He jerked in response, bracing for another thud to the head. None came. "There's a field road just up ahead on your right. Take it."

Dark was both impressed and perturbed that this human sack of shit had followed his directions without fuss. Impressed because everything had gone according to plan. And Dark was a man that enjoyed smooth goings. Perturbed because he hated to think such spineless men lived and breathed and bred.

The engine surged, and the Plymouth shot forward. Dark found immediately that he'd assumed too much, too quick.

Rocky leaned forward over the steering wheel. He had to know that he couldn't get far enough if a shot was fired through the seat, but he was almost far enough to evade another knock on the head. Almost.

Dark half-stood in the back and reached out and clubbed him once. The car slowed and veered first left, then right, only managing to hang on to the far lip of the road.

"Shit, man, stop it," Rocky begged, trying to cover his head and steer simultaneously.

"Stop the car," Dark thundered.

"Ok, Ok. Just don't hit me again." The car slowed and pulled as far off the side as possible without dropping into the roadside ditch.

"Now take the keys out and hand them to me." Rocky did as instructed. Perhaps that one meager flash of bravery was all he had in him.

Mr. Dark dropped the keys into a pocket. "Now get out." Rocky didn't move. "I see you're thinking again. That's not going to do either of us any good."

"Just tell me what you want. We can work something out."

"Get out."

"Fella, I'm not going anywhere until you—" Rocky was cut off once more by Dark. But this time, it wasn't a hard thump to the side of the head. No, this time, it was more penetrating. A small blade punctured the side of the neck, its tip slicing through the flesh and underlying muscle and tissue like warm butter.

"Holy shit," Rocky cried out. "What the hell?" he gasped. He grabbed his neck, and when he brought his hand away, it was covered in blood.

He hadn't paid any attention as Dark threw open the rear door, jumped out and opened the driver's door. He yanked Rocky out before the man even knew it.

"Don't worry, tough guy. There's plenty more blood where that came from." He dumped the big man on the dirt road. Rocky grunted and rolled over. He had a hand back on his neck where a puncture continued to leak. Dark held the knife out over him.

"Beautiful, isn't it?" Dark said, his focus on the weapon. "A relic of the first World War." Moonlight glinted off the blade's edge, but nothing more as the steel had been blackened as the soldier had to wield without notice. "The Mark 1 by L.F. & C.... whomever the fuck they were. Mean little bastard." And it was.

Six inches of blade on four inches of hilt. But unlike most knives, the handle was brass, with knuckle dusters the holder's fingers wound through. Each finger loop had a raised spike, and the pommel was a larger brother of those four spikes. It was more what one's mind would conjure when thinking of medieval European weapons than government-issued GI gear. But, in service for the better part of thirty years, the knife was one hell of a backup when more sophisticated modes of war ran depleted.

On the ground, rocky swallowed hard. The man was draped in some large black cape or robe. The easy breeze billowed the sides out like a balloon inflating. It would be comical except for the sinister gaze of those catlike, ghostly eyes and that awful knife in his hand.

"On your feet."

"Come on. I'm hurting here." Rocky was trying to catch his breath, to slow his racing heart. But the air was terrible, tainted. Something awful rode the wind.

"That's exactly the point, Rocky."

On his feet, barely, Rocky could not keep his mouth shut. He was no longer just scared. He was terrified. A man didn't walk you out to the middle of nowhere to throw you a beating. No, this seemed to be part of something much more permanent "What have I ever done to you, buddy? Mr. Dark and Scary? Huh? Hell, I don't even know who you are. Maybe I have seen you around, but I don't know you, mister." Rocky was scooting himself across the ground with the heels of his feet and the palms of his hands. "Is it Geraldine? Are you sweet on her? Hell, man, I can respect that. I ain't ever been one to stand in the way of true love." He was really groveling now.

Dark followed at a leisurely pace. Beyond the car lights, there wasn't another light in sight. Rocky had passed the field road only a quarter of a mile away, but the field had ended, and several hundred yards of prickly underbrush separated it from the next. The world was a very close, pressing thing.

"Take her. Hell, take her and the kid. I wish you the best."

Rocky slipped and fell down to the muddy ground. Dark moved closer and closer.

Then Rocky noticed something. He stopped backpedaling across the sediment and looked up to face his abductor. "Hey, buddy, what happened to your gun?" A smile started to sprout across his broad pasty face. "Guess you think I'm an idiot." Then, suddenly, he shoved himself up, finding his second wind and even a third gust.

"Guns. They have their time and place," Dark responded as he jabbed his foot out, kicking the rising Rocky. His foot was met with little resistance. Rocky crashed back to earth, cracking his skull hard against the unforgiving road beneath him. Mr. Dark stood over him. "But I'm a hands-on, roll-your-sleeves-up type of guy."

Rocky was almost knocked out. He was in the act of passing out as a brand new pain arced across his chest like a blazing trail.

Rocky cried out in pain. His shout echoed on and on. Incredibly, Dark now held two knives. Exactly alike. One in each hand. "Don't go blacking out on me, you fat fuck. I am not carrying you," Dark said.

"Please, God, stop it!"

"God has nothing to do with this. Nor even the devil. The misery you now suffer, you wrought by your own hand."

"How? What the fuck did I do?"

"Think, Rocky. If you are still able. If you ever were. Consider your sins. All of them. You have so many, but I'm not too worried about you fucking around with your best bowling buddy's wife or flirting with Nadine at the lunch counter. Or even when you have Little Mack punch your timecard at the end of the day when you decide a beer at the river beats a day at work."

Rocky was still, entirely and absolutely. His shaking, which he'd been unable to control since being hit the first time outside the house, vanished. "H-how did you know...how did you know about any of that? The fuck? Who are you?"

Mr. Dark and Scary looked at him. He loved this part. When his prey realized that, in some impossible, mind-bending way, they weren't being attacked by an ordinary man. They were almost scared to think beyond that. It was as if their minds hit a brick wall, unyielding and unwilling to consider they were facing down a real-life boogeyman.

"I am justice for Geraldine and Danielle, Rocky. I am vengeance for the weak. As you so eloquently put it, I am not sweet on her, but by ridding her and her beautiful young daughter of you, I'm sure she'll be sweet on me." Mr. Dark sneered. "I'm sure I'll be at the top of her Christmas card list for the rest of her life, Rocky." The sneer transformed, and he giggled.

Rocky said no more. There was a defeated look in his eyes.

Every time the man in front of him slowed, Dark slashed at his bare neck and head with the knife, punched him with the spiked knuckles or poked him deeply with the knife's blade.

It wasn't too long of a walk. Finally, after ten minutes, they made it to the end of the field road and the back edge of the field where brambles grew.

"What is that smell? Shit, it stinks here."

"Oh, that? I wouldn't worry too much about that." It was then that the first sounds from up ahead reached him. First, it was a high-pitched squeal. Then came the sound of hurried footsteps.

"Come on, man, Mr. Dark, what the hell is this? For fuck's sake, just tell me."

Dark did not.

They soon reached a barbed wire fence. Rocky walked right into it. Unfortunately, the moon was hidden behind clouds, and visibility was poor. He stumbled back where Mr. Dark caught him and, before pushing him off, reached around and sliced his throat wide open with the knife blade.

Rocky started forward, turned and looked at Mr. Dark with the oddest expression.

"I've grown weary of your company, Rocky." Rocky fell then, landing with a thud.

Mr. Dark stood watching him bleed out. He watched his lungs rise and fall and then rises for the last time.

He tore open the man's shirt. Buttons flew here and there. Dark didn't disrobe the man. He had no interest in seeing this sad sack naked. Instead, Dark let his blades fly free on his chest and stomach. The bleeding was minimal, with the heart stopped. Still, it oozed from the body in red frothy bubbles.

Rocky's body was covered in horrible slashes and jagged rips a few minutes later. Mr. Dark flipped around the blade and used the blunt end to tear the slash longer.

Mr. Dark stopped and stood straight. He was breathing heavily, and his face was coated in a thin layer of blood. Nevertheless, he was smiling, truly happy at his handiwork.

"All right, you bloated piece of shit. I think we're done here." He picked Rocky up as best he could and manhandled him over the fence.

On the other side, still out for the night, livestock moved and snorted. Squeals lowered into aggressive growls; the hogs started to trample each other to reach their surprise meal.

Thanks to the smell of blood in the air, the hogs didn't take long to find Rocky's body and descend upon their midnight snack.

The hogs belonged to Vernon Crockett, the most well-to-do of all the Crocketts out here at what everyone called Crockett Bottom. The family was infamous for miles around for once upon a time copulating with their own cousins and even siblings and for basically being lowlifes in almost every sense of the word. Dark had no intention of paying him a visit this evening. No, he was just here for the hogs.

Compared to Rocky, old Vernon was practically a damn saint.

The hogs did the hard work. And they got full bellies for their efforts.

Within ten minutes, nothing at all was left of Rocky. Even his work boots had been devoured.

Dark turned and began walking back to the car. Halfway there, he started whistling a tune.

Life was good.

9

THE RENAULT HOME was a large rambling house built years before the Civil War. Sheriff Sparkman felt he was inside a museum instead of a personal residence, with fine attention to detail and what looked like professional decorating.

However, Charles Renault's corpse lying at his feet reminded him that he was not on a tour of historical artifacts but at an active crime scene, a homicide, of one of the most prominent citizens in town.

The body was in bad shape. Sparky and Charles knew each other, of course. The sheriff had never been a fan of the guy, but he didn't think he deserved to die in such a way. The entire body appeared to be pulverized. Mashed and smashed, almost flat like a giant rolling pin.

"What in God's name do you think did that to him, Sheriff?" Roy Polk asked. Roy had been with the department for almost fifteen years, joining the force right after high school. A decent officer, he and Sparky had worked together back when Sparky had been chief deputy before his first successful run for the sheriff's job.

"I don't have a clue, Roy. I've never seen anything quite like it."

"Looks like he was killed here," Tom Harper said. He was dressed in street clothes and not his uniform, but everyone around knew him.

"Yeah," the sheriff responded, looking at the pools of dried blood around the corpse.

Sparkman stepped back and looked around. He'd been here all evening since leaving the mayor's office. It was dark now; it had been for hours. His stomach grumbled, remembering he'd missed both lunch and dinner.

"Roy, mind finishing up here?" the sheriff asked.

"Not at all, Sheriff. It shouldn't be too much longer now, anyway. I'll write it up for Chief Leavitt before morning."

Sparkman nodded his thanks to the deputy, waved to the others and walked outside, Tom Harper on his heels.

"What in the hell has come to Farmington, Sheriff?" Tom asked when they were out the door. The night air was cool, almost refreshing. And the sheriff was glad to be out in the open. He in no way suffered from claustrophobia, but something about another victim, another life taken, worked his nerves, and as the evening wore on, he could feel the walls closing in on him.

"I don't know, Tom. But whatever it is, it doesn't seem to want to leave on its own."

"Hard to run someone out of town if you don't know whom to target," Tom said.

Before Sparky could answer, the icing on the turd-flavored cake that day had become pulled up in front of the house. It was a black Lincoln and sparkled in the streetlights like onyx.

"Shit. The old man," Tom spat before Sparky could mutter the same idea in his own words.

"Knew he'd be here sooner or later," Sparky said.

As the Lincoln rolled to a stop, the driver wasted no time letting the car settle back down on its suspension before his door shot open, and he was in a blur of motion as he moved to open the back door.

Walter Renault was in his late seventies and looked like he felt every year in his few movements. Finally, he accepted the driver's hand and let the younger man haul him to his feet. He looked the part of a frail old man.

Sheriff Sparkman knew better. Much better.

"Sparkman," Walter Renault growled as he approached the two lawmen. He leaned heavily on a polished hickory walking stick he'd used since Sparkman was a senior in high school. "Just what in God's name is going on around here? Your receptionist Deputy Dumbass won't answer my questions. That hair-brained second-in-command of yours won't answer his telephone. So, I've dragged my elderly ass down here to see about my son, Sparky. What's happened?"

It was with that last that shame sparked on the sheriff's cheeks. He'd lost his head, worrying more about his own exhaustion and issues than being empathic for the real victims of the madman on the loose: those left behind to mourn their passing.

Whatever Sparkman thought of Charles' father, he was the man's—the dead man's—father. And there was no doubt the old geezer loved his son. He'd paved his whole life with golden streets and rescued him with fancy lawyers and well-applied pressure in all the right places. And sure, some of that might have been to save himself embarrassment, but the two were two of a kind, the only remainders of their once extensive family.

"Walter, I was just coming to see you."

"I'm sure you were, Sheriff. Sure, it was at the top of your mind. But tell me...Is Charles—"

"He's dead," the sheriff said. He did so gently so that Walter wouldn't have to say the words.

The old man looked like he had the wind knocked out of him. Sparkman took a step to catch him might he fall, but in the blink of an eye, his driver, Mel Hocum, who'd worked for the old man for years, was there, a hand on the old man's arm. Walter was a tall man and had been taller. Now he stooped, dependent on a piece of wood to walk.

"What happened? Accident? Robbery?"

"Don't think it was an accident. We can't tell if anything was taken. It doesn't look like it. But we can't be sure. We were hoping maybe you could help out with that…tomorrow. Or the next day."

"Somebody…killed my boy?"

"Yes, sir, I'm afraid that's what it looks like."

When he looked back at Sparkman, the sheriff swore the man sounded thirty years younger, full of piss and vinegar.

"Was it this rascal everyone's wagging their jaws about?"

"We can't say for sure, Walter. We—"

"Was it damn it? Was it this fucking lunatic you're letting run loose, spilling the blood of good God-fearing folks? Huh? Was it?"

"It's likely," Sparkman said. The outburst shocked him, but he didn't give the old man an inch.

"You hear me, and you hear me well, Sheriff Sparkman. You find this piece of shit. You find him now, god damn it, or you'll good and damn well wish you'd never pinned that nickel store star on your shirt." Walter was raging now, stabbing the air between them with a crooked finger, spittle flying wild.

"That sounds a little like a threat, Renault," Tom Harper said.

"Harper, this ain't none of your business. You don't have a horse in this race," Walter spat, turning from the sheriff.

"The sheriff is doing all he can. I hate it about your son. I truly do, Mr. Renault. But a man like Charles, he's made plenty of enemies along the way. We don't know anything yet. And we'd hate to let the man that took your son's life go free because we ran off half-cocked. We just don't know enough yet," Harper said.

"News flash there," Renault said, but he was calming. Sparkman watched it. Tom Harper was like that. He could stand toe to toe with the biggest jackass around and gain their respect. He was a natural peacekeeper.

"You get out there and find who killed my son, Sheriff," Renault said after a moment. "He's all I have…had."

Sparkman put a hand on the old man's shoulder. "He'll pay Walter. He'll pay for Charles and all these other folks he's taken too soon. That, I swear."

Walter shrugged off the hand and nodded his head. Sparkman

watched him, accompanied by Mel, walk toward the front door of his late son's home.

"You going to let him go in?"

"I'm not messing with him. He'll end up getting in anyway."

"Get you some rest. Hell, you've been burning the midnight oil for weeks. We aren't as young as we used to be."

"Don't I know it?" Sparky clapped Tom on the back, and they parted ways. Tom to his personal truck, Sparkman to his cruiser.

10

DORA JEAN TIMMS shook and shuddered at the sound of the back door opening. It was like an invisible hand, wide open with fingers spread. It pushed right into her guts, gripped unimaginably tight around her intestines, and began twisting without the slightest hope for relief.

"Dora Jean, where's my supper?" her husband called, in a less than tender tone, albeit with one she was pretty familiar with.

She turned then, smiling as best she could. Bile crept up the inside of her throat.

"It's in the oven, Mack. I'll warm it up for you."

"For once, it would be nice to have the fucking meal on the table when I got home from a hard day's work."

Dora Jean didn't know what to say, so she said nothing. Mack had been in one lousy mood after another for the last week. Worse than usual. She merely nodded and went and busied herself in the kitchen. Before he could say another word.

She could not stand wholly straight and moved with a slight limp. Mack didn't seem to either notice or care. Why would he? It was his fault.

She breathed a little easier when she heard the springs on the sofa accepting his body weight. She'd made meatloaf and mashed potatoes. It was Mack's favorite, and she well knew it. She'd prepared it all afternoon, even nicking her hand while peeling the spuds. But it had been ready hours ago when Mack should have been home.

And, of course, he was late.

He was coming home later and later these days. It would have been a relief for Dora Jean if he hadn't had such a wicked temper when he finally darkened the door. But there wasn't a whole lot she could do about that.

Mack ate his dinner without comment after she carried it and placed it on his TV tray. He paid her no mind. He just started shoveling it in.

That was how the rest of the evening went: Mack in front of the television, her in a chair next to the entryway to the kitchen. She sat almost at attention, should her husband of two years need her to fetch him anything.

This was not the life she envisioned when the two had married. After tying the knot, her aspirations were dashed rather quickly. They did not have a honeymoon, in her opinion. It was an awakening to a way of life she thought she was escaping when she left home, but even her father had never been as cruel as Mack Timms.

The night wore on, and the two spoke little, and when the time for bed came, Dora Jean was beginning to think things might be okay, if only for tonight.

"You going to wash the dishes or just leave them to draw roaches and gnats?"

"I've already washed up, Mack. I did it during your programs." He didn't respond. He only looked at her. Then finally, he grunted and pushed himself up off the sofa.

Dora followed him into the bedroom. She'd already turned the bed back and fluffed his pillow. Sometimes she thought she was raising a child instead of caring for a husband.

Mack turned before climbing into bed and stared her down.

"What is it, love?" she asked, trying to keep her voice even.

"Anything you want to tell me?"

'What do you mean, Mack?"

"Do anything today, anything out of the ordinary?"

Dora Jean began to tremble. Only slightly at first, but visible regardless, and Mack noticed. And she saw that he noticed, and that made the trembling worse. "I...I don't know what you're talking about, dear?"

Mack was not a big man. In fact, he was rather short, but he was heavy. Dora fed him well, and he ate just about anything put in front of him. In fact, Dora Jean was an inch taller than Mack, but that meant little in the grand scheme of things. This she had learned quite well over the last two years.

"I think you do, Dora." Mack placed his hand on his belt buckle and slowly unhooked it.

Dora Jean felt that twisting fist back in her gut. The belt was black cowhide leather. An inch and a quarter wide. The leather around the holes was worn and cracked. It made a rustling, whooshing sound against the denim of his work pants as he slid it free.

"Mack, no. Please," Dora Jean was urging as the belt came free.

"You know the rules, Dora. You don't leave the house without telling me first."

"I had to. We needed groceries. How do you think we get food in the house?" She shouldn't have said it. But, even as the anger flashed through Mack's eyes, she knew she'd made a dire mistake.

"I know how the damn groceries get here. I pay for them. I work all day long to make the money you so carelessly spend, but that's not what I'm talking about. And you know it."

He was right. She did. He wasn't talking about her quick trip to the market.

"I heard about your little conversation with Ritter. Heard ya'll be getting really close. Close enough to kiss."

"What?" Dora Jean asked, just to have something to say to stall as her mind whirred.

Mack Timms wrapped the belt around his hand twice. Then, the buckle end swung only inches from the floor. That small, innocuous brass mechanism brought a whole world of pain.

"I didn't marry no loose woman, and by God, you won't become loose, not while I'm around."

"Mack, it...it wasn't like that. Terry was leaving the market as I was going in. He spoke, and I spoke back. That's all. I would never go outside our marriage to cheat. I wasn't raised that way. You know that. I take our vows seriously."

"That all sounds really nice, Dora. I swear it does. But I don't believe it for a second. That bastard has had his eye on you since grade school. So first, you're going to get what's coming to you. Then, I just might go find ole Terry Ritter and give him a taste."

"Mack," Dora said, "you don't know what you're talking about. So what do you want me to do? Ignore friends and neighbors when they speak to me?"

"Well, he ain't no neighbor of ours, so he must be a friend of yours."

"I've known him since we were both ten years old. You just said that. But I married you, Mack, darling."

Mack moved closer. Holding the belt like a whip, he looked not unlike some awful, dreadful beast from some fearsome fairy tale. "You make it sound like that is some kind of grand prize. Believe me, you cheating cunt, it's not."

"Mack! I've never cheated on you! Stop saying that," Dora Jean shouted. She couldn't help it. Even knowing the consequences, she could not hold her tongue still. It was one thing for Mack to lay his hands upon her. It was quite another for him to disparage her fidelity.

His response was both swift and jarring. She saw him twist at his hips, rotate his upper body, and slash out with the belt. Dora turned, hoping it would hurt less on her back than her front.

The buckle stung, and the pain radiated from the impact point between her shoulder blades. She cried out, but it was useless. So was her begging that soon followed.

Mack Timms was like a man possessed. He smacked her again and again, the brass opening up lacerations through her clothes and crimson stains sprouting and growing.

11

TOM HARPER DROVE from Charles Renault's house through the downtown area. Roscoe's, the drive-in burger joint with the pretty girls on roller skates and cheap hamburgers, was doing gangbusters tonight. As he passed, Harper saw that just about every slot was filled, and the teenagers were having a blast, playing their music and hanging out with friends. Likewise, the Skylark drive-in movie theatre was filled almost to capacity, despite a double feature of hinky science fiction flicks. Tom was more a western fan and specifically a fan of John Wayne, the "Duke." He couldn't stomach the science fiction and horror that was all the rage these days.

His job held all the horror and outlandish scenarios he could stand.

His window was cracked, and a car pulled to the side with several youngsters playing rock and roll around it. Harper hated most of it but couldn't begrudge the younger generation for their love of it. Wasn't that the way of things? Each generation embraced the new, making it their own. So he supposed it was, and he couldn't help but get nostalgic for his bygone teenage years.

The late spring air was warm and carried the sizzle of hamburgers and hot dogs roasting. His stomach grumbled, but he'd not had time to eat again. He should head home, grab something out of the icebox and hit the hay. Tomorrow would come too soon, and he had the early shift.

Tom Harper had been assigned to Winchester County for over a decade, ever since making the rank of lieutenant. He liked it, no, loved it. He was a country boy himself. Raised just outside a little town like Farmington. Well, honestly, there weren't many places like Farmington. But his hometown of Corinth was small and straightforward, and most folks waved when you passed by. He'd really taken to this place and even more so when his father found some land on the outskirts to retire to.

Unlike most small towns, communities, and hamlets, however, life here in Winchester County was anything but boring.

It seemed the whole of Winchester County was where the waking world met both dreams and nightmares.

There'd been murders before. Of course, there are problems wherever there are people, but he couldn't recall when the guilty party had taken so many lives and remained mysterious.

But he had a good idea, if anyone could recall. He knew a man that could.

The Winchester County library sat several blocks east of downtown on a well-shaded section of Confederate Street. But, of course, it was closed, being almost ten o'clock at night. Harper didn't care; he figured there was a swell chance the fellow he sought was still inside.

The state trooper parked near the front entrance beneath the boughs of a white oak tree, stepped out of the car and walked briskly to the front double doors of the library. As he expected, most of the interior lights were off, with only a few here and there left on.

Lt. Harper rapped his knuckles against the glass door. The night was preternaturally silent around him, and his knocking echoed into the distance. Nothing happened for a few minutes. Then, just as he started to have second thoughts, a shape moved deep inside the building.

A few moments later, a man came into full view. He was an older black man, greying heavily at his temples. He wore a maroon cardigan sweater over a white button-up shirt and grey slacks. His feet shuffled as he walked, never truly leaving the ground.

His cheaters hung on a chain around his neck. After he placed them on his face, he peered through the darkness at Harper. Tom waved, and recognition brought a smile to the other man's face.

A few seconds later, he'd fished a key from his pocket and held the door open for Harper. "Evening, Mr. Harper. Out awful late, aren't you?"

"Sorry to intrude so late, Willie, but it seems crime never sleeps."

The old man, Willie Truitt, nodded sadly. "About that, sir, we can agree. How may I help?"

"I need a history lesson," Harper said.

Willie understood. Tom stepped in, and Willie took point and led them through the darkened space. From the doors, they walked past the reception check-out desk, out into the open area that housed tables, the card catalog and then on past the darkened towering shelves of countless tomes.

Harper was always a little intimidated walking amongst the books. But he also breathed in the smell of dust and aging paper. He was not a great student, and his entire high school career would have been utterly lackluster if not for sports. But he'd always enjoyed reading. Even in the last few years, he'd become a big fan of the western writer Louis L'Amour. He'd read his first novel, *Hondo*, over a weekend.

He didn't share his bookish nature with many. Tom Harper was a private man and kept to himself.

But with Willie Truitt, it was different. He'd been one of the first people Tom met outside the local government and law enforcement after moving to town. They'd hit it off on Tom's first visit to the library, and their friendship had grown over time.

Willie had been the head librarian for years, and Tom also discovered that he was the local archivist when it came to the stranger happenings that often went on around here. He also possessed a staggering knowledge of local history. Like a university professor, Willie could opine for hour after hour about the storied past of Winchester County, name all elected officials for at least fifty years, and give you great insight into the various tragedies befalling the town for at least a hundred years.

From a hard-working farming family, the Truitts were good as gold and highly respected around town. For a black family in the 1950's, that was saying something, Harper thought. He was smart as a whip but never spoke condescendingly and took extraordinary lengths to make what he said clear to those who didn't live their lives with their nose stuck in a book.

He was also closed-lipped.

Willie led him to an innocuous door at the rear of the library. He pushed it open, and Harper once again marveled at the space.

On a cheap, county-provided desk were stacked dozens of hardback books, sheaves of paper, a Royal typewriter, a green-shaded banker's lamp, and a steaming mug of coffee. The walls were adorned with old, yellowing charts, maps, and photos, some in frames, some just affixed to the wall.

This was not the inner sanctum of some uppity professor but where a man, intensely interested in the goings-on both present and past of his community, worked.

The two men took seats, Willie behind his desk and Harper on the opposite side.

"Well, Tom, what's on your mind?"

Harper leaned back in the seat. He exhaled slowly but said nothing. He was considering his phrasing.

"You'll forgive me, but you look plumb worn-out."

Harper gifted Willie with a slight grin and a quick eyebrows arch. "Guilty as charged, Willie. Guilty as charged." The getting settled on his words. "You've heard about the, well, the killings?"

"I have, sir. Hard not to."

Tom Harper nodded.

"What have you heard?"

Willie considered. "Just what folks are saying, I suppose. Feller is going around, in the dark, at night, murdering a couple of men, something awful." Willie laughed, but not a jolly sound. "But just what kind of awful, no one will really say. Seems the details are a little," he searched for a word and seemed to snag it out of the air. "Debatable."

Tom snorted and shook his head, slowly wagging it as a sad hound dog might. "They are unsettling. To say the least. But sounds like to what degree, no one has really caught onto."

"They may well be, Trooper. But I tell you, don't think that much matters none. Folks are spooked. And it seems like there's righteous reason to be."

"I ain't going to come here, ask for your help, and lie to you, Willie. I'm at wit's end, and no one else seems to have any idea how to tackle this."

"What about your state boys? You talked to them?"

"Sure did. For all the damn good it did. They figure I live close enough to lend a hand. But we need a lot more than that. This bastard is smart, Willie. He doesn't leave a trace behind. No one sees him coming or going. The only first-hand witnesses act if suddenly they are struck dumb, deaf and blind. He isn't a kook doing it for fame, I don't reckon, or it seems like he'd have gone public with something. And if it'll sell papers, I figure Jeff Kathy is waiting for that to happen with bated breath."

"You say the witnesses, they aren't any help? None at all?"

"Not a single one of them. I couldn't tell you if it was the damn Easter Bunny or Santa Claus."

"That seems odd," Willie said, and the springs of his chair creaked as he leaned back.

"Sure the hell is. I can't figure it out."

"How many eyewitnesses were there?"

"Four, as best I figure. But that may not be correct. I figure a few told us they didn't see shit but did. Pardon the language, Willie." The elderly librarian waved his concern away.

"What did the victims have in common?" Willie asked.

"What?" Tom asked, already lost in thoughts far away from here.

"The victims, Trooper," Willie prodded, "Why them? Did they share some sort of common thread? What is this guy's motivation."

Tom Harper breathed heavily. He leaned forward in his chair. He spoke calmly. "What I'm about to tell you is conjecture, half-brained theory, and spit-balling."

"I'm familiar with that particular method. I assure you." Willie gave him a gap

Despite himself and everything crashing down around him, Harper grinned. But it was short-lived. "This hasn't gotten out. And it can't. Once you hear what I say, I think you'll agree."

"Okay, Tom, you have both my interest and my oath of silence."

Harper nodded his gratitude. "Best we can figure, from whom all punched their tickets, they were...." Tom shook his head once, an almost exaggerated shake that looked like a child tasting a spoonful of spinach and said, "they were all putting their hands on somebody in the household."

Willie's leathery brow furrowed. "Putting their hands on, Trooper? As in beating on someone?"

"Yeah, Willie. In some cases, right rough. Roger Blevins used his kid like a punching bag. After we found Roger, the boy, Yates—and what a name that is, right?—was wearing a cast on his arm, won't tell anyone how it happened, and Roger's old lady won't say a peep. She had a few marks herself.

"Likewise with the other two's wives. But one had the eyes of a 'coon, and the other, I swear, smiled the whole time."

"Can't say I blame her if it's true." Finally, it was Willie's turn to shake his head. "That all these men were sadistically attacking those closest to them."

"Well, all that fit until tonight."

"What's happened?"

"Charles Renault was just found dead in his house."

That took Willie by surprise, and he fell back against his chair. "Princes Charles, himself?"

"Unfortunately."

"The old man been to see you yet?"

"Just saw him."

After a moment: "What doesn't fit with Renault?" Willie asked.

"He wasn't married. He had no children."

"That doesn't exactly mean he wasn't knocking the shit out of someone regularly, does it?"

Tom Harper's eyes widened as if a lightbulb had gone off. "Knowing Charles as we do isn't exactly out of character, is it?"

"Well, I'm not one to speak ill of the dead," Willie said, "but I understand the need for discretion."

"First, I thought it might be one of the victims. It could still be. But that doesn't hold up. Whoever is doing this is strong. Damn strong. So I'm at a dead end."

"What do you need from me?" Willie asked.

"Well, Willie, I was hoping some of what I'm saying maybe jogged your noggin of anything."

"You asking if whatever is going on now ever happened before. Like the same kind of killings?"

"I reckon I am," the state trooper answered.

"Tom, that's a 'might loaded question. After all, this is Winchester County."

12

THE TOWN of Farmington lay smack dab in the middle of Winchester County, itself located in the extreme northeastern corner of Mississippi. The Great Kansas Southern Railroad cut through the town's north edge on its way, slicing a diagonal line across the whole county. At the intersection of two major routes, Highways 54 and 27, the town grew into a healthy retail and business trade thanks to the three most essential things in real estate: location, location, location.

But like most things, there's a dark side to this idyllic small town. But, unlike most other places, the dark side of Winchester is like a deep-rooted and saturating stain that can never be washed away.

Founded in early 1836, misfortunes accompanied every step forward, almost as if some curse had been set upon those early settlers. After those first lean years, what followed was more than anyone's fair share of psychos, bad seeds, and general human garbage lashing out at a world they no longer believed in. If they ever had in the first place.

Some would say that's just life. Nothing anyone can do about that. Some places are worse than others, and the world keeps on spinning.

But in Winchester, an additional element is often involved. In the middle of the twentieth century, folks don't often discuss it in polite company even now. But it's there, infused with everything and everyone. Occasionally, there's a pulse, an eruption, an event that crosses from the hard, cold reality into the fiery realm of the supernatural.

In Winchester County, the stuff of legends walks hand in hand with daily life. But, unfortunately, most often, those walks are not strolls of delight on a fair summer's day but harrowing excursions into frightful and sometimes devastating destinations.

There are no clear answers as to why.

But there are records. Thanks to Willie Truitt and a few folks like him, preserving the strange, macabre history of Farmington and Winchester County.

"Hmmm," Willie said after a minute of thought. He put a finger up and rose from the seat behind his desk.

"Give me just a moment. I need to check a few things."

"Sure, no problem." Harper watched as Willie shuffled around the office, a bit sprier in his step than before. The old man enjoyed his work, even when the subject turned so glum. He also seemed to employ his own filing system. Metal filing cabinets sat around the office, but a whole mess of papers was stored outside the cabinets. Most of the papers were stacked in columns, and it was in these that Willie spent a few minutes thumbing through.

Willie Truitt flipped through paper and grunted, groaned, audibly tsk'ed, and cursed under his breath several times. Tom knew better than to rush the elderly man. While he was more knowledgeable than any other citizen in local lore, he did have his quirks. The state trooper was not about to rush the process.

After what felt like an eternity, Truitt said excitedly, "Aha, found it."

The old man shuffled back to his desk, a thick ledger in his hand. The book was made of maroon leather, now cracked from age and must've weighed close to five pounds. Dust billowed up as it smacked across Willie's desk.

The librarian opened the tome, licked his index finger and began shuffling pages. Then, after a moment, he settled on what he was looking for.

"Find something?"

"Seems so." Willie straightened his glasses and began poring over the handwritten words on the page.

"Back in '08, almost fifty years ago. Then, a string of murders similar to those you described occurred across Winchester."

"Tell me about them," the trooper urged.

Willie consulted the pages in front of him a bit longer, then scooted closer to his desk, looked up at Tom and began.

"August of 1908, Farmington wasn't much more than a small but growing community with about two hundred souls. This was long before the railroad. The old cotton gin was still going strong, but not much else. Times were hard and lean.

"Three men were killed in the space of a week—August 9th through the 14th. At first, they all seemed random, with no single thread connecting them. That is until the sheriff at the time, Gordon Brinkley, took a closer look into each man's goings-on and family affairs.

"You have to remember this was a different time. Then, most folks were of a much more independent nature than now. Folks didn't share what went on behind closed doors. Even less than they do now, and they surely didn't like talking to the law, any law, that came poking around.

"No offense, Tom," Willie offered.

"None taken," he said. "Don't worry about my sensibilities, Willie. I know how most folks feel. Just tell the story."

"First victim found was Clyde Stewart. He lived over in what they called Cherry Hill back then."

"The Matchsticks."

Willie nodded. "Yes, which most folks call the Matchsticks, now. Well, old Clyde was a family man. Married with three kids, all girls. When he was killed, the girls were 12, 10 and 7. The wife turned the other cheek as he…fiddled with his own daughters." Willie shook his head in disgust. He looked back at the pages before him. "His wife found him about two hundred feet from the back door. Wasn't much left. He was all chopped up."

"Chopped up?" Tom asked. "Like with a knife?"

"No. Most folks seemed to agree it was with a scythe."

"Hell."

"Fitting," Willie said. "The wife wouldn't say anything about her husband bedding her daughters. I guess for obvious reasons. He was dead now and could do no more harm. The oldest girl, well, she finally told it. But the way it's written here, no one believed her. Put it down to the mad ramblings of a child just losing her father.

"But the second victim, well, everyone already knew he was one foul fella. Christopher Miller. Went by the name Crooked Chris. Had some type of disability. Made him carry a cane and gave him an odd-looking walk. I'm not sure why that information was recorded for posterity, but it was. Seems he was quite the local character. Didn't work. Depended on handouts, which I'm guessing back then, weren't very much. Never married and never even left his mother's home. After the father died, it looked like he became the man of the house. The only thing was, he had a mean streak a mile wide. Now, being all crippled, he couldn't do much more than run his mouth in public, which he did on every occasion. But his poor ma. She was quite an old lady by this time. Christopher was in his forties, and she was in her late sixties, in bad health.

"All her life, she'd been a devout attendee to the Baptist church, the only church in town, for many years. Then, she began coming to church with injuries and bruises and had become as meek as a mouse. Folks were curious, I'm sure. But you know, Farmington, they talked more amongst themselves than with the old lady. So then, one Sunday, she just didn't show.

"Before anyone could do anything, Crooked Chris went and got himself hung from a tree and beat all over. His whole body was bruised, and bones were broken. They never decided for sure, maybe a baseball bat or a boat oar. But see, the hanging didn't kill him. The rope was long enough to torture him, restricting his breathing and ability to cry out."

"So he was alive when he was bludgeoned?" Tom asked.

"Yes, sir. I'm guessing that was the intention. He felt every bit of it."

"Damn."

"The third, well, is a bit stranger."

Harper shook his head. Exhaustion, confusion, and worry leeched away his energy. "Let me have it."

Willie did. The trooper sat there and listened. Willie was right. It was a strange case and one that Tom couldn't as quickly shake off as the other two.

"They found the killer?"

"I can't tell you for sure. There's a bit of a question on that. Oh, they brought in a suspect. But it never made it to trial. The fellow they collared for it was Joseph Cutter. He was a shopkeeper at Dixon's General Store before Randy's opening up in the '20s." Willie rechecked the notes. "Cutter was not an imposing man. He was short, plump, and some said a bit retarded. He was a stocker, never ran the register and couldn't take inventory because he couldn't count past ten. He did not fit the part, did he, Tom?"

"No, detective," Harper answered, working up a slim grim at Willie. "He does not. Doesn't sound like he'd be physically capable of hauling around men. Don't matter what size man. It's not an easy thing. How were they so sure of this...Cutter was their fella?"

"Found him covered in blood at the scene of the third crime. Seemed he was knocked out and didn't regain consciousness before the cops showed up."

Tom nodded. "Convincing."

"The more delicate and scientific policing methods have not been so long in vogue as you remember such days. But, honestly, it was the easiest thing for everyone involved. A time for peace, maybe?"

"The easy way out, I have seen it. Sometimes it's the only way out. But if you grab this guy, throw him on trial, and the murders continue, you'd look a little green at the gills, I'd say."

"They did stop. Nothing else even similar to these specific incidents in all these years. Until now."

"Why didn't he make it to trial?"

"He died. In a cell. Ruled a suicide…but…."

"Somebody probably helped him," the trooper concluded.

"Exactly." Willie closed the book. "With the suspect no longer among the living, the whole thing was quickly swept under the rug. And as I said, the killings stopped, and things went back to normal."

When Willie finally finished, they both sat silently for a moment.

"I sure do appreciate it, Willie."

"You're welcome, my friend. Hope it helps."

"I know more than before I got here, so I reckon it can't hurt."

"Good luck, Trooper," Willie said as Harper stood to leave.

"Thanks, Willie. I'm going to need it."

13

MARK BORDEN WOKE early before the sun lit the sky. He was exhausted and felt feverish. But he couldn't miss work. So he threw the covers off of him.

The last few weeks had been a wrenching, fearful time for him. Mark didn't understand what was happening.

But he did have nightmares.

They were awful things, vivid and visceral. Mark didn't dream often. When he did, they were usually happy dreams. Dreams of his father, or at least the sight of him, just knowing him from old photographs and of his mother. Dreams of his childhood before he had to step out into the world and become a man.

But lately, they were dark, scarier, and more realistic than the waking world. They came nightly. Each night, he woke either screaming or sweating profusely, sometimes both.

And he remembered them, at least for a while after waking.

Last night had been one of the more gruesome ones.

He'd been working, mopping the second floor of the courthouse. It was late afternoon, and red sunlight filtered in through thick-paned windows. He was in a hallway halfway between two sets of offices. The corridor was eerily silent. No murmurs or hushed conversations came from the office doors, as they were all closed shut tight. From downstairs, where sometimes shouting and screaming accompanied those paying local taxes, was likewise tomb quiet.

Mark could hear the swoosh of the wet mop over the aging tiles. The slosh of water from his bucket sounded especially loud in the hallway.

A soft, tender cry reached his ears.

Mark stopped abruptly. He held the mop handle in his hand. Mark strained his ears. No other sounds came. Mark turned and looked. He was still alone in the hallway.

Feeling a little silly, thinking the sound may have been due more to his wandering imagination as he worked than to some child in distress. Nonetheless, he moved closer to the office doors closest to the rear of the corridor, which ended at the door leading to the stairwell.

He knew the people these offices belonged to, of course. The one on the left was Mr. Ketchum, and Mr. Howell was on the right. He didn't know what they did, but he knew they wore ties to work, which meant they did something important. Moreover, they always acted busy, with hardly a word to Mark when they passed. He put his ear to each door but heard nothing on the other side.

Odd, they usually worked at least until five, both of them. Mark looked back to the window. The tint of the light had not changed, and suddenly Mark wasn't sure of the time. He never wore a watch. It got in the way as he worked. There was no clock in the corridor, but surely, he wasn't working over and not realizing it. Or was he?

He heard the child again just as he stepped away from Mr. Howell's door. It was low and weak but unmistakable. It was that of a small girl. She wasn't speaking. She was crying.

The sound was not coming from either office. Mark moved before the sound died away. It was coming from the other side of the stairwell door. Mark's shoes fell heavy on the floor, and the footsteps echoed on and on.

Mark stopped and placed a palm against the heavy door. He

listened closely, but the sound was gone, vanished. It hadn't faded away but simply ceased. Mark felt a little silly and looked over his shoulder to ensure no one was there. He was still alone in the corridor.

But what if the little girl was in trouble? What if he could help but chose not to? Could he live with that kind of guilt? Even Mark's mind, underdeveloped compared to the average person, or maybe because of it, had a huge heart and couldn't help but emphasize those in need.

He pushed open the heavy door. The stairwell was dim but not dark. Mark could scarcely make out the stairs. One flight went up, another down. Mark was a fan of neither dark nor confined spaces. He always used the elevator while working and only entered the stairwell to sweep it out once a week. He dreaded it every single time.

But now he had cause to enter and search. "Hello," he called meekly. There was no answer. "Is anyone in here?" Again, he was answered only by silence.

Mark was really feeling foolish now. He turned and started to walk back into the corridor.

"Help me," a fragile voice called. It was clear and ringing but low and distant.

"Where are you?" Mark called, but he started down the steps before waiting for a reply.

"I'm down here. Please hurry."

Mark did just that. He started taking the steps two at a time, and before he realized it, he was on the bottom floor. No one was there.

"Help," the voice called again, and he pushed out through the exit door into the full light of day.

And it was déjà vu all over again.

The sunlight had changed. It was no longer the dying light of the late evening but the golden rays of morning. Mark swallowed hard.

He saw her, not the child, but the young woman. She was there on the bench, just like always. She turned to him, but her face was gone. Instead of a charming smile and twinkling eyes, her face was a mess of ruined flesh, blood, and viscous fluid.

And then he awoke, repulsed and afraid and screaming.

Mark wasn't much of a drinker, never had been, but he swore he felt as hungover as a regular alcoholic on Sunday morning.

He wasn't in the mood for a shower. Which was completely unlike him. He could hear his mother in his ear: "Cleanliness is next to godliness, my sweet Mark. And we all want to be close to God, don't we?"

In the bathroom, he relieved himself and moved to the sink. He splashed water on his face. That was his go-to on the rare mornings when he went against his mother's advice and skipped his shower. It helped in sluicing away the previous night's sleep.

When he looked into the mirror, he did not recognize the face that looked back. But, of course, even though he knew such a thing was cliché, that mattered little.

Mark had always considered his face friendly, if not handsome in any way. But what looked in on him from the mirror's reflection was entirely different.

"What's the matter? See something you don't like?" Mark stumbled back in shock. The voice that came from his mouth was not his own. Not even close. He saw his lips move, but the voice was from somewhere else.

"Who, who are you?" Mark asked, never taking his eyes off the face in the mirror. Instead, he watched in morbid curiosity as the face came closer, looming larger in the mirror's frame.

"Why Mark, don't act like that." The face in the reflection was a mockery of his own features. The nose was sharper, the cheeks gaunt and the eyes, dark slits that revealed nothing of the soul within but shone with a color Mark had never seen in the natural world. The face had an expression of scorn and distaste as if he couldn't stand addressing Mark. "I'm you, the better version, you might say. The you that isn't afraid of a soft breeze or some pencil-necked public employee that couldn't make it working for the private sector. No, you are a lamb, my dear Mark. I am the wolf."

"Stop it! Go away!" Mark slammed his hands over his ears and shut his eyes. He backed into the wall and slid down until he sat on the floor. "Please, please go away," he pleaded.

Mark wasn't sure how long he remained that way. But sometime after, he opened his eyes. The only thing he heard was the blood rushing in his ears.

He stood up and hurried out of the bathroom. He never once looked back.

14

RICHARD, what she'd taken to calling the rooster she could hear, crowed. As it had the morning before and the one before that, she counted the mornings as the rooster crowed. She hoped he was well-trained and only crowed at sunrise. If not, her figuring might not pass muster.

Kathryn was like that. Even at the tender age of ten, she was well-studied and possessed an analytical mind. But *she* didn't know that. The woman that brought her here. She was not concerned with who Kathryn was. No, she was more concerned with molding young Kathryn into some perverse toddler-like thing.

But it was morning. That was good. Mornings were good for a while. There would be breakfast. Never anything much more substantial than oatmeal. But it filled the empty recesses of Kathryn's stomach. The warm milk was another thing. She did not care for warm milk.

When the woman came in to feed Kathryn and the two other girls held in pens, she said nothing. Only left a bowl of oats and that darned warm milk in her wake. The woman who wanted to be called Mother was dressed in a housecoat and had her hair up in curlers. Kathryn had stopped pleading with her when she came in.

The young girl had already learned her lesson. There was nothing but derision and cruelty when they were out here. Inside, where they were allowed to dress in the clothes Mother laid out for her, it was different—if she behaved.

The three girls were in, from all appearances, a barn. There was no livestock, but there was hay stored within eyesight. Four pens, cages large enough for a full-grown man, sat in a row. Plywood had been slotted between them to keep the girls from reaching each other or seeing their faces. But they could talk, and they often did.

If the rooster could be trusted, Kathryn had been here at least a week. Seven long, awful days. It was impossible to see outside to know the time of day. But that was her best guess. The girl next to her, Melia, had been there, she said two weeks, but the girl was younger than her, and Kathryn wasn't sure she could take her at her word. Not because she was lying but because she was probably confused and terrified. The other girl, Wendy, had been there the longest. She didn't say much. She talked a little when Kathryn first arrived but had become almost mute. Kathryn knew almost nothing about her.

Her belly growled, and she moved over to the oatmeal. It was already cooling, but she shoveled it in with the provided spoon like it was going out of style. It was hard to keep it down. Her stomach stayed in distress, and the only place to use the bathroom was the sage in which she was kept. She'd wiped her bottom with hay for days. But still, she ate.

She and Melia talked a little after breakfast. They tried to engage Wendy, but the girl remained silent. Finally, the two girls talked about their families and how much they missed them, stopping short of tears.

The morning whiled away, and the barn got warmer. When the door opened again, Kathryn drew a breath and held it. She scooted on her bottom to the very back of the pen, praying that she would not be chosen.

When Mother placed the key in the padlock of Kathryn's cage, she wanted to cry out for her real mother, her real father, but she knew silence was not just golden but wise in this situation. So, likewise, she did not shy away when Mother reached her hand out to her. Instead, she offered her own, swallowed, and finally exhaled as mother pulled her from the pen.

She didn't hazard a glance behind her as Mother led her out of the barn, across a bright sunny day, to the back of the house. Instead, she looked around without moving her head, scanning with only her eyes. She always did this. She wasn't sure why, but deep down inside, she knew that if she collected every detail and paid attention to everything around her, she would have a better chance if the opportunity to escape ever presented itself.

The house they approached was one story, low but long and wide. It was a solid brick house with green shutters and a big front and back yard. She could see no cars parked in the drive as they approached the back door.

As they stepped into the cool house, Mother placed her hand over Kathryn's eyes and led her to where she wanted her. This was something Kathryn had also become accustomed to. For some reason, Mother preferred concealing most of the interior of her home.

They stopped as Mother opened the changing room closet and shoved Kathryn in.

"Hurry up, Jolie, our tea will get cold," Mother called through the door rather unkindly.

Kathryn shivered, not from cold but from repulsion. She had no possessions. Not even the rubber bands she wore in her hair. She wore no jewelry. The clothing she'd been wearing, when taken away from life as she knew it, was long gone, replaced by a sad-looking thing that was more a sack with a hole at each hand and two on the sides, leaving her shoulders bare.

She'd been wearing her favorite dress that day. It was new, and she'd worn it every day since Mother, her real mother, had returned home from Morrison's with it. Mrs. Morrison's shop was the only store of its caliber in town, and there was no telling how much she'd paid for the garment in that swanky place. It was a beautiful navy blue with a white satin runner bisecting it near the hem and a thinner but matching runner below the neckline. It didn't have a bow, and she was darn glad of that. It would have ruined the whole thing. No, it was perfect as is. It looked good with her black patent leather shoes and white socks with lace.

The dress was no doubt entirely ruined, even without the bow. Thrown in the trash, most likely. It was gone, as was everything she'd ever known. Here, in this awful place, she had nothing, not even her name left.

--

A LITTLE AFTER NOON, SHERIFF C.W. "SPARKY" SPARKMAN WAS BALLS deep in Jeri Ann Williamson. During the time they danced beneath the sheets, all thoughts of murderers and even of the victims and the survivors disappeared. It was his time now.

He needed relief, for he feared he might just have a spell or mental breakdown without a moment's relief with the awful things eating away at his brain.

What was not awful was the feeling of Jeri Ann beneath him. He needed something, someone, and this young brunette, with the firm, powerful twenty-two-year-old body, fit the bill perfectly.

The sheriff was married and had been for many years, but he was also a man with both needs and desires, or so he told himself. So if his beloved wife refused him her lawful duty, he saw it as no great sin to get it from someone else.

And Jeri Ann certainly didn't mind. She was making it with the sheriff. That was a big deal for a young girl.

She could do things his wife could not or would not.

They were out of town, just across the state line into Tennessee, about twenty minutes from the heart of Farmington. The State Line Hotel, while the name was undoubtedly nothing original or creative about the name, accurate as it was, was notoriously close-lipped about its guests, and Sparky had always been a man that appreciated discretion.

Right now, he was a man that appreciated the extra bit of time Jesus spent on the female form.

"Oh, Sparky," Jeri Ann cooed. "You're such a devil," she breathed into his ear after pulling him to her. Her hands gripped his bare buttocks and ground him into her deeper, harder. He wasn't about to complain.

Later, when they were both spent, Sparky watched her dress. He couldn't help but smile.

"You work tonight?" C.W. asked. Jeri Ann looked over at him and winked.

"I just worked. But yes, I'm going to work tonight. Gotta pay the bills somehow."

Sparkman nodded. "Guess the guys would be awfully disappointed if you didn't show up." Jeri Ann worked evenings at the Tasty Freeze, and it was no secret that men a few years older than the average customer base made special efforts to patronize the establishment when Jeri Ann was on the clock. C.W. couldn't blame them, not at all. She was a looker with her dark hair, tanned skin and athletic physique.

But that didn't mean he didn't hold some resentment; at times, his skin turned the worst shade of envy green. Besides the star he wore on his chest, he didn't have much to offer a young girl like Jeri. And he well knew it. He damn sure couldn't announce that she was off-limits. After all, he was a married man, and a scandal like that would be well remembered by voters in the next election, and as much as he liked bedding the hot thing, he was not prepared to give up his career and play house with her.

Yet, thinking about her in the arms of another man made him grit his teeth and see red. But he let it pass. He didn't want to ruin the last few moments the two had together today. With everything going on, who knew when the next chance they'd have to get back together would be?

"Sparky," she said in that whiny little voice that could move mountains and change minds. Then, fully dressed, she sauntered over to him. A little swing in her hips and little sway in her walk. She smelled terrific, even beneath the musk of sex and sweat. "You know you're the only man for me."

He smiled and nodded, knowing it was nothing but a kind lie and hoping she didn't turn the tables on him. She'd done it before, bringing up his wife, and she would probably do it again. Thankfully, she didn't this time. Instead, she straddled him again, her dress allowing her legs to stretch accordingly. She found his reawakened member, and before he knew it, he was coming again, even as they were involved in deep wet kissing.

They said their goodbyes, and she gave him a quick kiss on the cheek and left. He took his time putting on his clothes. They had arrived separately and with a gap, and they left the same way. Never could be too careful, even here.

With the day's heat crushing down on him back in his cruiser, guilt tickled at Sheriff Sparkman's mind. He couldn't help it. He'd been raised better. He had never planned to become an adulterer, but damn it, a man had needs, didn't he?

His two-way car radio went off as he hit the Farmington town limits. Thankfully, his chief deputy, Wilemon, answered before he had to. It wasn't anything serious, a fender bender down by the general store. No need for him to hurry, so he didn't.

He took his time navigating the town streets. Mid-afternoon and the retail sector was bustling. He passed the courthouse, and his eyes lingered over the bench where Florence Webb had sat. He frowned without realizing it.

Out a side door, the janitor, Mark Borden, was beating rugs from some of the offices. He'd slung the rugs over the iron banisters and swatted them with what looked like a tennis racket. Big puffs of dust wafted up with each swing.

The cruiser idled its way on down the street. Soon enough, he pulled his car up to his usual parking spot at the back door of the sheriff's department.

Sparky stepped out, pushed the car door closed, turned, and looked face to face with old man Renault.

"Sheriff," the elderly man started, "I've come down to see you myself. Seems I can't get you on the phone."

"I've been out in the field. Investigations do require that."

The old man's ruddy face deepened a dark scarlet, but he kept his words even. His driver was beside him if the man's cane proved insufficient to keep the old geezer upright. "Well, then, Sparkman, can I assume since you're now back, you've put the investigation to rest and are readying yourself to arrest the man that killed my boy." But, while the words were indeed even, the taunt was still evident.

Sparkman was about to reply, a remark that would cost him dearly, but thankfully the back door shot open, and Chief Wilemon was there. "Sheriff, there you are. I need you in here."

C.W. Sparkman didn't smile, he knew better, but he was profoundly relieved. "Coming, Chief," he said. Then to Renault, "Sorry, duty calls." And with that, he turned and left the man there, fuming and huffing.

15

NIGHT COVERED THE LAND, and the ground let loose the heat it had absorbed throughout the day. An hour after darkfall, the air was cool and sweet. Crickets sang in the distance, and a big, waning moon hung in the sky. More than anyone could ever count, stars spread like a glittered velvet blanket across the heavens.

It was a good night for murder.

Mr. Dark was outside the window, watching events unfold. He enjoyed the coolness of the night.

Inside, raised voices raged. Something shattered against a wall. A woman screamed, and a man shouted. A door slammed, and everything fell quiet.

Then he saw his cue. Like a moving, living shadow, he left the window.

Victor Mint stepped out onto his back porch. The house was outside town limits and faced a massive field in the back. Corn was reaching skyward but was still months from maturity. A thick cigar jutted out from between his clenched teeth. He was still dressed from work but had loosened his necktie. He knew Lepher Jenkins was behind on his payments. Victor had set the machine in motion to start foreclosure proceedings next Monday. Then, the land could be had for a fraction of its worth. There would be no shortage of bidders if it ever came to auction, which Victor would not let happen. He was already making plans for the land. Sometimes, it paid to be president of one of the biggest of three banks in town.

He fancied being a gentleman farmer, like his daddy's folks before him. As a matter of fact, horticulture was a keen hobby of his. His large garden took a lot of his time, but he felt it was worth it. He had the most magnificent tomatoes in all the county. Probably anywhere else, too.

Victor was immensely proud of his garden.

In one hand, he held a small glass of whiskey. His other hand, he opened and closed, working out the soreness in his knuckles. Victor could only imagine the pain that smart-ass wife of his would be feeling. That thought made him grin.

Suited the cunt right. She got exactly what she deserved. He thought she would cry herself to sleep in a few minutes, and then finally, there would be peace in the house.

He stood there, looking out and sipping on his drink. He felt like a new man now. Sometimes, you just need to flex your muscles and deal with the problems in life with a bit of old-fashioned aggression. It worked wonders.

He took one last draw of his cigar and looked over to his garden, situated beside the left side of the house and running parallel to the road in front—so everyone could see his pride, joy, awe, and wave as he tended to it. The successful businessman and his garden. It would be perfect except for the rest of it, the family.

Roberta, his wife, was the last one left. And he was getting damn tired of keeping her around. But he had to wait. It couldn't look suspicious.

Victor tossed the cigar to the side and turned back in when he stepped on something. Something squished beneath his shoe and the deck. Victor looked down and saw a dark stain, but the deck fell in the shadow of the house from tonight's moon.

He moved back to the door, opened it without looking and switched on the porch light. The deck was a mess, covered in thin, runny liquid. Juice. It was tomato juice. Though dozens of the plump red vegetables were now only smashed husks.

And they were not just tomatoes. They were his tomatoes. His prize-winning 'maters!

Victor bounded down the steps and ran over to the garden. Even in the dim light of the night, he could see the broken stakes his tomato vines had been strung to broken halfway up—all of them. The other vegetables were in bad shape as well. Everywhere he looked, root vegetables: radishes, turnips and the like had been haphazardly yanked from the ground. Melons, both watermelon and cantaloupe, lay about smashed and burst.

Victor Mint had never been a man to keep his temper in check. Seeing his pride and joy, his most special thing in the world, defiled in such a horrendous and careless manner took him to the heights of anger.

The glass of expensive whiskey had been all but forgotten in his hand. Then, suddenly, he needed it.

Just as Victor brought the glass to his lips, something hit him squarely between his shoulder blades. The glass cracked against his teeth, and he shot forward.

He let out a curse but was more concerned with breaking his fall than verbalizing his anger. He almost dropped to a knee into the plowed earth. Instead, he spun around to see what had happened. If that damn bitch had snuck out and hit him with something, there would be hell to pay.

There was no one there. Nothing but darkness. Bewilderment struck him hard. He glanced to the left, right, and all around. But, again, there was nothing, no one there. But...that was impossible. He didn't just imagine the shove. Did he? Of course not. He wasn't crazy.

But he sure felt silly.

Then the darkness shifted right in front of him. Shadows swirled. Victor had never seen anything like it. It was a strange sight to behold, like black tissue paper folding in front of him. He would have chalked it up to the whiskey had he not felt the wind from it.

Victor took small, baby steps backward toward the house.

"Where you going, big boy? Something spook you?" Victor twirled. The voice was deep, clear, and close, but he still saw no one.

"Who the fuck is there?" he demanded.

He looked back at the door. It seemed far away, though it was probably less than fifteen feet away. He considered sprinting toward it. If he could make it, shut it behind him, shoot through the kitchen, he'd be within reach of his gun cabinet.

He didn't get the chance. Something solid and hard slapped across his cheek. He saw nothing, but the blow rang his bell, momentarily deafened him, and caused his eyes to water.

He stumbled, brought his palm to his cheek, and tested the tender flesh. It hurt like hell.

"Show yourself, you damn coward."

"I thought you'd never ask," the voice said, and out of the darkness, a figure emerged. Clad in black, with a fearsome face and hateful eyes the color of piss. Victor shrank back in fear, but only for an instant. "

"I know you," he said quietly, then more loudly. "You're the damn mop pusher down at the courthouse." The knowledge gave him some type of second wind, some sort of brazenness that he had not exhibited before. While disoriented by the phantom blows, Victor knew this man's face, and the man he knew was no threat.

"No. Sorry. You may know the face, but you don't know me." Before Victor could react, his attacker slammed a fist into his throat, and he went down—hard. "Fathers, lock your doors. Mothers, hide your daughters. Mr. Dark and Scary has arrived," the stranger called out and then laughed like he'd said the funniest thing of all time.

Dark moved over to him and kicked him three times in the ribs, breaking more bone with each successive kick. Victor raised his hands defensively, but the gesture was futile.

Victor tried to roll over and crawl away, his whole right side ruined. However, a kick to his ass knocked him back to the ground.

Then Mr. Dark began to giggle, a high-pitched and crazy giggle.

"I've seen some sorry excuses for men, Vic, but you, my friend, take the cake."

"Please, please. I've had enough," Victor said, much more humbly.

"Scratch that; you take the whole bakery." He giggled once more at his joke. Then: "Now, on your feet."

Victor was squirming on the ground. His whole body cried in pain. How had that bastard been so strong? He was little more than skin and bones—a skin sack, his daddy used to call it.

"Stop it. What the hell did I ever do to you."

"Nothing. You're not man enough to do anything. Not to a man. That's the problem for weak, scared little boys like you. Striking out at those weaker, those softer than you. Well, I'm here to tell ya, Vic, you're my bitch tonight."

Victor covered his face. The man in black reached for him.

16

THE POND WAS about a hundred yards west of the Mint house, in a little corner of property the greedy bastard had been able to carve off his opposite neighbor to the Jenkins farm: Rudy Coln.

The banks were tended, and the grass was cut low to deter slithering serpents from hiding in wait for prey or innocent passerby. Dark hadn't toted Mint that far. Instead, he'd used Mint's old pickup that he kept out in the garage. Like the pondside, well-maintained but rarely used.

Well, that wasn't necessarily true, now, was it?

Mint had used the pond just fine. For his sick, aberrant acts.

Now, too, would Mr. Dark and Scary.

There was little concern Mrs. Mint would investigate her husband's doings when she heard the pickup crank up at this odd hour. No, Mr. Dark witnessed the punishment doled out to her tonight. As long as her husband had his attention on something else, it was not on her.

He parked the pickup truck just off the rise of the bank and killed the engine.

In the bed lay Victor Mint. Very much alive but not enjoying life too much at the moment. Dark reckoned that almost every prominent bone in the man's body was broken, smashed, cracked or bruised. Plus, a few minor bones to boot.

The prominent banker was as docile as a newborn kitten when Mr. Dark slipped him from the truck bed and tossed him roughly on the ground.

"Up," Dark commanded.

"I..I-I can't."

Dark looked down at him. Pathetic. Mint looked like shit. He was on his back; his right leg lay at an awkward angle. His left arm flopped below the elbow.

"Are you such a weakling you can't even take to your feet? How could the likes of you ravage those poor souls even weaker than you? Does it make you feel like a real man, Vic? Do you feel powerful, in control, the master of your universe, to control by your sheer iron will and the skin of your knuckles?"

"Fuck you," Mint spat at him as strands of blood gushed from his mouth, pouring over his lips in some cases, straight through the air in others. "Fuck you. You're nothing but... a scrawny janitor... you're nothing. You are beneath me."

"Nasty mouth you got there, Vic. But sticks and stones, as they say. Sticks and stones. I've seen a whole lot of sorry excuses for people, Vic. And your torture and subsequent slow death will be... immensely satisfying for me."

"What?" Victor demanded. But he was no longer looking at Dark. Instead, he looked to the sky above as the dark man pulled him forward into cool, low grass that the dew was just beginning to kiss.

DARK WAS LEARNING. HE WAS CALLED TO THESE PEOPLE BY SOME unknown means. He knew everything there was to know about them and about those they turned their fists on. He was unsure how it worked and figured it didn't matter. He had a purpose. He had a mission. And that was enough.

He was getting stronger, too. With every kill, his power grew. Then, it was beginning to feel just like old times.

The pond was like dark onyx in the night. Its placid surface was as still as a sheet of glass.

"Why are we here?" Victor Mint asked. Barely. He had little fight left in him.

Mr. Dark dropped the man's feet, and Victor grunted.

"Don't ask stupid questions," Mr. Dark said. "You know fucking well why you're here, you detestable piece of cow shit."

Victor only stared at the pond. Didn't reply. He couldn't. Dark watched as the total weight of realization pushed down on him.

Through the darkness, crickets chirped, and night birds sang. Nothing else could be heard. No traffic, no human sounds. It was as if Dark and Victor were the only two people left in the world.

"It was an accident," the man on the ground finally said. "I swear." The last words were said lowly, almost as if he were speaking to himself.

"Two accidents?" Dark asked.

"Yes. I tried to save them," Victor pleaded.

Dark looked out over the pond. "Don't reckon you tried too hard?"

Victor looked up at Mr. Dark and Scary. There was hate in his eyes, of course, as well as pain. But there was something else. Dark peered closer. Remorse. Yes, that's what it was. But was it remorse for what he'd done, or was it more for getting caught? Of course, Dark knew the answer. It was always the same.

Men like this didn't regret what they did—or if they did, they only did so when caught.

"They were children, Victor. Just kids. With their whole lives ahead of them."

Victor had rolled over and crawled away at a pace that would make a snail laugh. Dark watched him for a few moments. He was a pitiful creature, but a creature, nonetheless. A monster.

Some would call Dark a monster, but he disagreed. He was here because of these actual monsters. These monsters doled out pain and punishment to those in their charge. It was a father's responsibility to care for and protect his children. Not end their lives in some cornfield pond more suited for the cows than children.

Dark stomped down. Victor's left hand crackled under the shoe heel. He shouted, and the sound echoed off into the distance.

"Scream, shout, cry out all you want, Vic. Really clear out those lungs. Scream until your own eardrums burst. There's no one to hear you. The closest person is your wife. And do you honestly think she'd come to see about the man that put her two children in the grave and used her as a god damned punching bag?" Dark was shouting by the end of his rant.

Victor appeared to be using his feet, as much as he could, to move now. But he held his arms and hands tight against himself, unwilling to sacrifice them. It was almost as if he were trying to screw himself down into the earth beneath. As if his body was a drill bit and he would penetrate the sediment below.

A fool til the end.

Dark gave him a moment. Either to regain hope or simmer in his own misery. Either would be just fine.

Mr. Dark swept his black robe back and bent low to grab Victor by the collar. Victor made strange strangling noises as the shirt grew taut around his neck. He waved his arms as Dark lifted him off the ground quickly, without much fuss.

He brought Victor up to eye level and lifted him even a little higher.

"Tell me. Tell me what you did."

"You know, you already know," Victor managed, averting the other man's eyes.

"I want you to say it. I want you to part your pretty dick-sucking lips and tell me. If not, I have plenty more ways to hurt you, to bring you pain you never thought possible."

"No, I can't." Victor was crying. The tears were really flowing.

"Cry me a bucket, asshole." Dark threw Victor over his shoulder.

Again, he took the weight with little effort. His shoes crunched through thick grass as he neared the water's edge. Here the bank's lip was only inches above the pond. Dark didn't stop but continued walking out through the water. The crunch of the grass underfoot was replaced by loud splashing.

"What are you doing?" Victor asked in a panicked whisper.

After reaching chest level, Dark dropped him from his shoulder, and Victor crashed into the water. He was flailing even as he hit. Before he could drown or swim, Dark was pushing his face down toward the pond's dark bottom by the neck. He held him there.

Somehow Victor found the strength to struggle, but there was no use. Dark held him tight. His attempts to free himself, draw in air, and even breathe were sloshing the water, creating large waves and drenching Dark.

Air bubbles began breaking the surface.

"Shit, boy, you're acting like a fish out of water. Ha! Get it?" Dark giggled and yanked Victor's head out of the water. The bank executive gasped for air. He sucked it in quickly and started retching.

"Now, I'm asking you nicely. What did you do?"

"They drowned," Victor said at length. Then, with an exaggerated gesture, Dark threatened to dunk him. Instead, Victor grabbed Dark's bicep. Not to stop him, he had already given up on that, but to plead and then say, "No, please, it was me."

"Tell me how," Dark said. "Step by step. I want to hear it."

Victor nodded slowly. He was still trying to catch his breath. "Okay, okay." He sucked in more air. Snot covered his face. "They were playing out back. Between here and the house. Both of them. Vinnie, the boy...was playing with a wooden sword. He always did that. Janice, my...my daughter...she was playing with dolls. I was tending my garden. They just wouldn't shut up...they... called for me. Wanting me to play. I didn't have time. I had things to do. The garden—"

"Oh yes, you're precious garden. Isn't much to look at now, I'm afraid."

Tears welled in Victor's eyes.

"The little bastards just got to you, huh? Pressing on that last nerve, as they say?"

"Yes, yes," Victor said, eagerly agreeing. "Something just came over me. A moment of weakness. I thought, my god, the things I'd be able to do without those pestering children."

"Uh-huh. So, what did you do, Victor?"

Victor Mint said nothing.

Again, Dark submerged him. This time, Dark waited until the fight died away and slowly pulled him back, free from the water. Instantly, Mint began gulping in large mouthfuls of the cool night air.

"I drowned them," he said flatly between swallows of air. "I called them to the pond and suggested we all go for a dip. They thought I was crazy, of course." Dark said nothing. "But it seemed almost a mercy to them. Like it was God's work." This time Dark did snicker.

"If that's so, Victor, I think I like my God better than yours."

Victor just looked at him.

"Pushed their little ole heads underwater like I did yours, didn't ya?"

Dark could see Victor Mint's throat work as he swallowed.

"You did, didn't ya?" Dark cackled then, high and long.

"Look, mister, I'm sorry. Just let me be, all right? It was insanity, an awful moment of it. I swear, I'll turn myself into the sheriff first thing. Soon as I...soon as I see about myself."

"Insanity, you say?" Dark pulled Victor close to him. He could smell the stench of smoke and whiskey on Vic's breath. No telling what that bastard could smell. "What did they say as you plunged their youthful noggins beneath this shit-infested water, Victor?" His words were precise and even, his cadence smooth but slow.

Mint trembled. He shivered and quaked. He shook his head, his eyes closed, his mouth drawn back in a silent scream.

"Tell me, Victor," Dark repeated. This time he was cooing as if to an infant. "Tell me everything."

When Victor still said nothing, only continuing to impersonate a human fault line, Dark went to tip him back into the drink. Just the slightest movement was all the persuasion needed.

He told him. He told it all. In a combination of narrative and broken, awful mewling, the father told of how he murdered his children for the crime of nothing more than being children. He also told of how he planned to kill his wife when the time was right. It might be a year or more, but he would wait. For now, he'd seen that beating her into silence and servitude to her husband would suffice.

As long as he got to work in his garden.

His garden.

His motherfucking garden.

"Did they beg for their life, Vic? Did your kids plead for their pa to save them?"

"Yes," the miserable thing that had been Victor Mint said and exploded into more sobbing.

"What did they say?" Dark was boiling beneath his flesh, but this part required composure. He would need to remain calm and collected just a bit longer. "Their words, Vic. Their words?"

"Vinnie was the one. Janice just screamed to high heaven. It was my boy, Vinnie, he called to me, he pleaded with me. He said, 'don't, Daddy, don't. We love you, please.' And then his mouth filled up, and so did his lungs, and he was gone."

"He wasn't gone, Vic. He was dead. Snuffed out by his own pa. Sure is a tragedy for both of them kiddos."

Without another word, Dark had his trench knife in his hand. The blade hovered just over Vic. Mint had just enough time to draw in a sharp breath, and Dark struck him. Twice. Once in each lung. Unseen in the darkness, blood oozed from the punctures, mixing with the pond water.

"There we go. Try holding your breath now," Dark said, pushing Victor down. The man attempted a struggle, but he was beyond any threat now. Dark stood above him until air bubbles no longer breached the pond's surface.

The night was quiet. Nothing stirred. Nothing moved.

17

TOM HARPER SHOULD HAVE BEEN in bed hours ago. He went on duty at six a.m., mere hours from now. As a man of forty-four, he was tired. He'd worked an entire shift earlier in the day and had several more to go before a day off. But he knew any attempt to turn in would be futile. So instead, he'd spend the night tossing and turning as he had for the last several weeks.

Tom had confidence in C.W. Sparkman. He seemed a right-smart fellow. And being a sheriff was more challenging than being a highway patrolman. But, on the other hand, maybe it wasn't as dangerous, and you could cut yourself some slack when you were the head guy. Which, in Tom's mind, was the problem.

This wasn't a time to cut any slack, especially yourself. This was when you had to come out, both guns blazing, canvas the town, take in information, investigate like there's no tomorrow, for perhaps for some unlucky soul, they may not be one.

It wasn't just the murders. And it wasn't just Farmington. There had also been a rash of missing children in the neighboring counties.

After hearing what Willie Truitt had to say, his mind just wouldn't stop. So, for the sake of a clear conscience, more than the duty of his oath urged him to take to the streets and see what he could see.

And so far, he hadn't seen shit.

Mostly, he stuck to town. Up and down the quiet streets of Farmington he went. The radio was his only companion and drowned out the dull thudding of tires across the asphalt, that singularly hypnotic sound that could lull you to sleep despite its irritating grate on the nerves.

Only a handful of businesses were open past ten on a weeknight. So, he was at a loss after making multiple checks on the Skylark, which was often called the passion pit for the debauchery of local teens, and the drive-in diner. Then, finally considering heading to the house and hitting the hay, he ultimately made a right at the intersection instead of letting a left take him on home.

Patsy Cline's "Walking After Midnight" coming on the radio was the deciding factor. God, if that woman didn't have a set of pipes on her. Tom was a little long in the tooth to be falling for pretty singers on the radio, but Patsy, well, she was unique. A proper lady with dark lustrous hair and eyes that sparkled like diamonds.

With no one in the car with him, Tom's cheeks warmed just thinking about her.

Taking a quick trip up to the state line and back would allow him time to enjoy the song. Then, of course, he could drive home and idle in his driveway, but that would just be stupid, he thought.

The window was cracked a few inches. His old car sped faster as the storefronts fell away to houses and even thinned out. Beyond the homes lay the vast farmland of west Winchester.

The headlights of Tom's car cut gold ribbons through the night. Light clouds of dust blew over the road.

Patsy had finished her walk, and Tom wasn't familiar with the next song, but the crooner had a good voice, so he left the dial be.

When the two-legged form popped up farther down the road off to the right, caught in the lights, looking like a mere shadow of a man, a startled Harper swerved to the left.

The car shot by the silhouette. Tom took as good a look as he could as he flew by. Something caught his attention, and an alarm blared deep inside his mind. It grew unbearable by the time his foot slammed down on the brake.

Rubber barked and skidded on the asphalt.

Tom's head banged against the headrest.

Just as the car came to a halt, it was reversing. Tom's hand reached for the gun in the passenger seat. He spun the car around by its back end. The engine revved as Tom stomped the pedal and slammed the tranny into first gear.

The man he was approaching had already broken out into a run. The motor whined like a beast and was pushed to its limit.

Past the thin shoulder of the road lay a deep, broad ditch. The running figure could easily launch himself down but certainly not across it. By doing so, he would momentarily evade Tom but trap himself with little time to climb out.

Like a large majority of the population, Tom was right-handed. Shooting was not really a skill many people could be ambidextrous with. But he didn't plan on shooting the stranger without warning, at least not yet.

With the pistol in his left hand and the steering wheel in his right, Tom's car surged forward and bumped the dark figure. The form stumbled, and Tom stopped the car, engaged the parking brake, threw the door open and jumped out.

"Hands up, State Police," Tom yelled. On the road, in front of the car, the form rose and started running. Tom pointed toward the heavens and let loose a warning shot. The gunshot cracked through the night like pissed-off thunder.

"Stop, damn it. Or the next one goes right through you."

THE CAR HAD COME OUT OF NOWHERE. DARK CURSED MARK ONCE more for not owning a car. He was facing away from his pursuer. He could have turned and taken the man's head off, but he did not.

Tom Harper was a good man, a decent man. Despite having a

gun at Dark's back, threatening to add an orifice to his body, Dark felt no rage toward him. This was not a man that turned his fists to those weaker but used his strength to help those in need.

Much like Dark. Just nowhere near as effective.

Dark cursed under his breath. Of all the times to run into a decent fucking human being.

Dark's right hand twitched.

MARK OPENED HIS EYES TO A STRANGE SIGHT. A DARK ROAD, FIELDS OF corn and soybeans to his left and right. Pale yellow headlights washed over him from behind.

Mark's knees turned to rubber, and he dropped.

His forehead broke out in perspiration. Footsteps, heavy and fast, behind him.

Someone kicked him in the back, and he fell face-first into the asphalt. His forehead caught most of the impact, and he heard his skull crack against the harder road.

"Wait, wait," Mark called. But rough hands were on him, pulling his arms, twisting them against his lower back. Mark was not a physical man, and there was no way he could defend himself. He didn't know where he was or who was attacking him. The last thing he knew, he'd fallen asleep at his home, in his bed.

Obviously, he had not stayed there.

Handcuffs tightened around his wrists. The metal clicking caused something sick to grow in his stomach. The cuffs tightened down until the bones burned.

"Please, I don't know what's going on. Please," he pleaded. The man said nothing. He rolled him over, and Mark recognized him immediately. "Mr...Mr. Harper."

The man above him, holding a gun only feet from Mark's face, also seemed to know him. He looked confused. Almost like he wasn't sure who, or what, he was looking at.

"Jesus Christ," Tom said. "You're, hell, you're the damn court-house custodian."

Mark said nothing. He should have. This would have been the time to spill the beans. But he had no idea what to say. The last thing he knew, he was clutching his pillow. The next, he was here, wrestled to the ground and restrained.

Mark didn't recognize what he was wearing. It was black and baggy but didn't look like anything from his closet.

Then, in the glare of the car's lights, he saw the blood. It covered the unknown garment. Suddenly, he knew he had done something terrible.

He felt Harper's hands patting him all over his body and stopped when he found one knife and the other. He found an opening in the black robe and pulled them from Mark. Mark hadn't been aware he had anything on him. He caught a glance as Harper slid them into the back pocket of his pants. His father's knives from the war. Why did he have them?

Mark didn't resist at all after that. He was roughly pulled to his feet. Harper was speaking to him, asking him questions. Mark's lips only trembled, never parted.

Tom escorted him to the car and secured him in the back. Then, without dallying, he jumped behind the wheel, and Mark watched as the darkened fields started to roll by out of the window. After a few minutes, Tom Harper apparently decided his charge would not be answering any questions and fell silent himself. There was no other side beyond the hum of the tires on the road and the wind blowing in through the driver's side window.

Mark glanced in the rearview mirror as they passed the first streetlights leading into Farmington. It didn't look like him. Not at all. Dark, dried blood covered half his face. His face was drawn, narrow.

He suddenly remembered the face in his bathroom mirror. Now, he was wondering just what kind of trouble that bastard had led him into.

18

LITTLE KATHRYN WAS SLEEPING FITFULLY after counting sheep for hours. Resting was difficult, and actual sleep was almost impossible. Yet, she was not nervous or terrified for a second of her life. Sometimes talking with the others helped. But, often, it did not.

When the door to the barn creaked open, Kathryn's young heart jumped into her throat. Since her capture and detainment, Mother had never entered the barn this late at night. Not a single time. For the briefest moment, Kathryn considered it was not Mother but someone coming to save her and the others.

When Mother sauntered into sight, her hopes were dashed, and she mentally chided herself for giving life to something as silly as hope in this awful place.

Kathryn could tell quickly that something was off about Mother. She noticed it first in the way she walked. She was not sure-footed at all, almost like she couldn't keep her balance. Then she saw the glass jar in her hand and knew it was what her pa drank on weekends.

Mother was dressed in her nightclothes and had a despicable look on her face. But, if Kathryn was honest, she would have to admit that Mother was not an ugly woman. In fact, she was rather attractive.

But not tonight.

Now, she wore a long, thin gown. Kathryn could see clear through the material when Mother stepped directly between her and the light. She carried the hooch that Kathryn had always called moon rays or moon shine around the house. It was powerful stuff. It sent daddy straight to bed every time. Well, almost every time.

One night, her real mother was spending the night with her sister because her husband, Kathryn's uncle, had come down really sick, more than Kathryn's aunt could bear alone.

Her ma and pa had an argument, but momma took off anyhow. So she was left behind with Daddy. In other circumstances, it would have been routine and fine. Her daddy often watched after her when mommy wasn't at home.

Well, her daddy had been down in the dumps and pulled out some of that old homebrew he kept in his shed.

And he drank half the night. Kathryn knew because she snuck out to check on him. And best as she could tell, he drank two or three jars of the awful stuff. And he'd muttered to himself. Finally, he'd built a fire and sat around it, sometimes standing, others barely keeping himself upright.

Finally, when he'd had his fill, he settled on the ground in the backyard. Kathryn was more scared of him in this condition than at any other time in her life because he acted like an insane man. Dancing and singing under the light of the moon like a madman. Or somebody that belonged up at Mar's Hill. She chose not to try and wake him and get him to bed. So, she did the only thing she could. Kathryn quickly sprinted into the house and brought a blanket and pillow upon her return.

He roused as the young girl tried to tuck her father into the ground with a throw and a sofa cushion.

"Is that you, honey?" he asked.

"No, Dad, it's me, Kat."

"Oh, kitty-kat, thank you," he said as he felt the blanket upon him and pulled it closer. His words were slurred but calm and even. Kathryn didn't detect any of the threatening aurae she'd earlier felt on her initial trip out.

She had been relieved. She had never feared her father since that night. But just as she was about to leave him, he grabbed her arm. "You know I love you, kitty-kat? Right?"

"Of course, Daddy," she replied just as quietly and calmly.

"It's the only reason I haven't run that whore of a mother of yours out of town. It's because of you. But sweety, even a father's love has limits." All of that was delivered in a sleepy monotone that chilled Kathryn exponentially more than his earlier erratic behavior and gave her chicken skin all up and down her arms. It also broke her heart in a way it would never mend. Because apparently, her father's love had run dry just a few short days later, and he was gone. One year ago.

Not one letter. Not a postcard. No visit. Not even a phone call.

So maybe this Mother was right. Kathryn might just need a new mom after all. And one day, maybe a new daddy.

"I see you're awake," Mother said to Kathryn. Her words sounded strange and slurred. Kathryn wasn't sure how the older woman came to that knowledge. She'd closed her eyes as soon as she'd seen Mother and her haphazard attempt at walking. She'd been still, yet something had betrayed her. "Mother knows these things, Jolie. Now quit playing possum, and let me look at you."

Kathryn was unsure what to do, so she did as she was told. She opened her eyes and scooted closer to the pen's front.

"That's it, darling. Let Mother see you."

When she went for the lock, Kathryn froze. There, of course, was no posted procedure for how life went out in the barn. But in Kathryn's limited experience, Mother did not play with her daughters at night.

When the pen's door swung free, Kathryn considered making a run. If there was ever a time she could make a clean getaway, this would be it. The woman was deep in the 'shine, as her daddy put it, and she could hardly walk straight. But something about the woman stopped her.

In her time, she'd come to fear Mother more than she'd ever fear another human, and that fear gave her pause. Then, suddenly, her chance was gone. Mother snatched her up out of the pen. She about popped the girl's arm out of the socket. The calm that pervaded when talking a moment earlier was gone entirely, replaced by something darker and more hostile.

Kathryn made the mistake of crying out. Mother's response came quick. A stinging open palm across the girl's cheek quieted her.

"Jolie, you will not make a fuss," Mother scolded.

Instead of leading her out of the barn to the house, Mother led her to a table near the back. She instructed Kathryn to sit. The girl did so.

"Elbows off the tabletop," Mother told her. Kathryn removed them. She should have known better. That was one of Mother's rules. But, then again, Mother had many rules, and it was hard to keep up with all of them.

Mother sat down across the table from her. She plopped her jar down, and the contents jumped and then settled. Kathryn stayed silent and just looked up at Mother. The woman looked tired and sleepy. With her hair mussed and her eyes only slits now, she looked much older than she actually was. Nothing was said as she took another sip from the jar.

Kathryn's bottom lip trembled, and she felt that familiar burn in the corners of her eyes, letting her know that tears weren't far behind.

"Jolie, Mother needs to tell you something," she began. The woman sat up straight and brushed her hair from her face. Kathryn hated to admit that Mother did not look the same without makeup. In fact, she looked almost like a hound dog snagging sack beneath her eyes and

pale complexion. "There is only one Jolie. Poor little sweet Jolie. She made me so mad. No, you made me so mad. But that doesn't matter now." Mother seemed confused and unsure. Even accounting for the alcohol, Kathryn believed something else was at play. The little girl still didn't trust herself to speak. She had no idea what to say, and begging to go back to her pen would not work. No, whatever Mother had come to say would be said.

Mother went to pick up her jar but seemed to think better of it and left it be. When she turned her eyes back to Kathryn, her eyes were wider and looked clearer.

"Jolie was a beautiful girl. She really was. An angel." Kathryn nodded nervously. "But there was only one. And there can only be one now."

Something in those words carried dread and smacked Kathryn full-on in the gut. Panic began to grow.

"Mother," Kathryn said gently. "We all love you. We can all be Jolie. We want to make you happy." Of course, it was lies, but young Kathryn decided she had to say something. Mother's words were ominous, and she felt she meant to cull the litter, as it were.

Mother smiled sweetly, and it changed her face. "No, dear, that can't be right," she said. "There can only be one Jolie."

Kathryn knew what that meant, somehow. There were three of them, and that was too many. As much as she wanted to believe that two of them would be returned to their homes, that was a foolish line of reasoning. Even at her tender age, she knew that. No. There would be no happy reunions for those not considered good enough to *be* Jolie. Instead, they would be disposed of quietly and buried somewhere their parents or loved ones would never, ever find them.

And the third girl would be Jolie. Maybe not disposed of, maybe not buried, but lost just the same.

Before Mother could say more, a sound panicked her instantly. A car was approaching. Mother jumped up from her seat at the table and grabbed Kathryn once more by the arm.

"No," Kathryn said and tried to pull away in a unique show of defiance.

Mother paid her no mind, and her grip remained tight. Still, Kathryn tried to fight. Mother had no time to deal with her. She kept her hold on her and rushed her back to her cage. Kathryn couldn't break loose, and before she knew it, Mother was pitching her into the pen and locking the door before Kathryn could make her way back to the door.

The car stopped outside, and Mother turned, forgetting her jar on the table, and hurried from the barn.

At first, Kathryn had allowed herself to hope that maybe it was the police outside and they would all be rescued. But just like thinking earlier, Mother was some trench-coated detective in a funny hat, smoking a pipe, come to usher all the girls to the waiting arms of their parents. She was ultimately disappointed.

Kathryn waited but only heard the car door open and close, and then maybe the muffled, muted sound of a house door doing the same. She heard no excited conversation. No demands by police officers to come on out with her hands up. No, none of that. Just silence and that always present fear now amplified by Mother's words.

Kathryn finally fell asleep hours later, wondering who the new Jolie would ultimately be.

19

According to current Mississippi law, Mark Borden could be held up to forty-eight hours in police custody without being charged with a crime. After that, he was free to go. Come hell or high water, there would be charges, the sheriff promised. Resisting arrest. Fleeing an officer, etc.

At first, Tom Harper had brought him into a small room with a table and chairs and talked calmly to Mark. He told him about the murders, which, of course, Mark knew about. If working at the courthouse was good for anything, it was hearing the latest local grapevine droppings, but when the state policeman told Mark that he was now their prime suspect, Mark was floored.

He wouldn't hurt a fly.

Heck, he couldn't hurt one, even if he tried.

Tom went on to admit that he wasn't sure that Mark had anything to do with it. Said he didn't fit the mold, whatever that meant. Mark assured him that he was innocent of those heinous crimes.

But when the policeman asked Mark what he was doing out there in the middle of nowhere, dressed in a stolen judge's robe, with two very sharp war relics, covered in blood that obviously hadn't come from him, Mark had zilch to offer him.

He couldn't lie and tried to tell the truth, but he was at a loss.

If that had gone poorly with Tom Harper, it sure as heck fire went sour after the sheriff arrived.

On a personal level, Mark had never thought much of the man elected to the highest law enforcement post in the county. He never could put his finger on it, exactly. It reminded him of those bible salesmen who always used to come around, and his mother despised him. Not that she was against the bible, mind you. On the contrary, she was a God-fearing Christian her whole life. No, she said they marked those darn bibles up and tried to make a fortune of the Lord. She called them greasy. That was the feeling Mark got when he looked at the sheriff. And while he couldn't say why he had harbored the feeling for years.

Even though Tom Harper had said there was no evidence yet to link him to the crime, the sheriff yelled at him as if he'd watched Mark murder the folks in cold blood right before him.

"You don't have to yell, sheriff," he finally said. "I'm not deaf. I hear just fine," Mark said as kindly and humbly as he could.

Mark had never seen a human being's face transition through so many shades of red. It would have been hilarious if not so absolutely frightening. But, in Mark's opinion, Chief Wilemon, the sheriff's right-hand man and a much more decent fellow, snickered as if Mark had told a joke.

But there was nothing funny about Mark's situation.

"Now you listen, and you listen good, Borden," the sheriff said. He was still yelling but not as loudly. But unlike Wilemon, he did not look amused. "We have one good suspect for four murders, probably more, we'll find out soon enough, and you're it."

"I've told you, sir. I didn't do anything. Nothing."

"Maybe getting hit by that car knocked something up here loose," the sheriff said, pointing to his temple with a finger. Mark knew what he meant but didn't take the bait. He'd been called retarded, stupid, and even crazy all his life, and he found fighting such allegations only tended to make things worse. "I mean, that would probably fly in court. Insanity. Might just get you a one-way ticket up to Mar's Hill instead of death row down on the farm. That's better than a killer deserves, in my mind. But the law is the law. So is that what happened, Mark? Did that accident a few weeks ago mess you up in the head?"

It had been like this ever since the sheriff had stepped in. He had no time for Mark's side of the story. Mr. Harper had told him he'd get a lawyer to defend him, but it didn't look like he'd be showing up tonight. And no one seemed to be brave enough to intercede on his behalf. Even Tom Harper sat off in the corner, quiet and listening.

"What would a guilty man say? Huh?" the sheriff asked. When Mark didn't answer, the sheriff railed on. "Exactly. That is exactly what a guilty man would say." Then the sheriff looked down his nose at him as if a confession was forthcoming. It wasn't. Mark might not have been the sharpest tool in the shed, but neither was he the dullest. He knew better than to admit to something he didn't do. His momma had taught him that. And seemed like good advice here.

That didn't stop the sheriff, of course. He felt like he had his man and wasn't about to let anything jeopardize that.

As the night wore on into the early morning, Wilemon left the interrogation room, and so did Tom Harper. With him and Mark in the room, the sheriff calmed a bit. He was tired, as tired, at least, as Mark. With his thumb and forefinger, he rubbed his eyes constantly.

When Sheriff C.W. Sparkman finally admitted to himself that Mark would not incriminate himself, he opened the door and called for a deputy.

In less than five minutes, Mark was thrown into a cell, and his handcuffs were finally removed by a gruff, unfriendly man in uniform. He was told his jail-issued jumpsuit would arrive in the morning with the day shift. When Tom brought him in, they'd taken pictures of him and removed his outer clothing. The black judge's robe still mystified him, but he had no idea where he'd gotten it. It had been among the thousand or so questions he'd been asked and had no answer for.

While they allowed him to wash the blood from his face, they'd confiscated the robe but left him with his undershirt and his drawers, and that's all he had on now. It hadn't been so bad sitting at the table in the interrogation room, but now, sitting on a lone bunk in the cell, he felt exposed. He went for the bedcovers but realized his mattress was bare. Perhaps those, too, would be furnished by the day shift.

Mark waited to see if anyone would return to his cell. No one did. The cell connected to three more, all empty. Housed in the back of the sheriff's office, the holding cells were pretty much out of sight, out of mind.

It was dim. His escorting deputy had flipped the lights off as he walked out. He never even looked back at Mark. Mark didn't like the dark, and he felt chilled.

Despite his exhaustion, Mark had no idea how he would get to sleep. Over the last few weeks, sleeping in his own comfortable bed had been hard enough. But, in this sparse, awful environment with a lumpy mattress, he didn't even try.

Instead, he sat there, thinking. Without his mother to protect him, the world had its way with him, just as she'd always feared. She'd said it since he was old enough to remember and had made him promise to be good, always do as he should and stay away from bad people, places and things. He'd tried, but they had finally come for him anyway.

Mississippi used the electric chair, he knew. And he also knew that without a miracle, he would ride the lightning, as death by electrocution was often referred to.

Mark didn't have a hope in the world.

20

C.W. Sparkman sat in his chair in the den. He sat there looking out as moonlight silvered the lawn through the window. He had many things on his mind, and he hoped the whiskey he sipped would help clear his thoughts.

He'd been sleeping deeply when the phone rang tonight. It was Settlemires, the night shift deputy. Tom Harper had brought in Mark Borden, the county employee that kept the courthouse clean. Borden had been covered in blood and wearing what Settlemires had called a judge's robe.

It was like a gift from Heaven above.

A rare and unexpected blessing of both fate and fortune.

Mark Borden. Not in C.W.'s wildest imaginings had he ever considered that the old dummy would be involved in the murders that plagued Farmington this last spell. Although, to be honest, if not for the blood he was found covered in, C.W. would have thought Tom was having him on, playing some cruel, odd, tasteless prank.

But that same blood, damning as it might be, didn't tie Borden to the slayings. And it wouldn't. They would need more evidence.

But what C.W. really wanted to pin on him was the lost girls. Eight girls over two years had gone missing from the neighboring counties of Alcorn, Tishomingo and even McNairy up in Tennessee.

None from here. That would have been much too risky.

Looking back, that just might have been the only thing done right. The whole scheme sure as hell hadn't been thought out ahead of time. Unfortunately, very little planning on the front end had caused quite a few pesky problems along the way.

It was stupid. Stupid. Stupid. And C.W. Sparkman had no one but himself to blame.

The girls already hovered around the same age: ten years old. While each had distinctive traits and unique charms, they shared common attributes. Each had dark hair, either brunette or deep brown. They were all slight children, thin but straight and tall. All but two had green eyes. Those two with brown eyes had not lasted long. They all spoke softly, and seven of them were well-behaved.

His heart ached for them.

He and Tom had some words as Sparkman left the interrogation room. Harper had been waiting on him in his office, nursing a pot of stale coffee. Tom wanted to know why he'd handled the suspect so roughly. Sparky couldn't believe his friend had questioned him the way he had. He had no right. And Sparkman had said as much. Tom had said some things, but C.W. was already heading out to his car.

Borden had worked him up, but he had no patience for Tom Harper second-guessing his methods. The state police were already a problem, and having one constantly in his business was maddening, especially now.

C.W. did not consider himself an evil man. A weak man. A pathetic soul. Yes. But not an evil man. But as the days went by, it was harder and harder to tell himself that. If he was candid with himself, the way a man could only be in the wee hours of the night, life heavy on his heart and more than a touch of whiskey to lead him along, he had become an evil man, indeed.

The girls weren't for him. Sparkman had never understood the perverse attraction some men felt about young girls. That sort of thing didn't sit well with him. No, C.W. preferred his women full-grown. And boy, how did he? His mind strayed to young Jerri-Ann. While he was more than twice her age, she certainly was no child.

But he had a wife, and he could not, *would not* leave her. Jerri-Ann was a spectacular piece of ass, true enough. But such asses came, and they went. His marriage was for life.

It was nothing out of the ordinary, the way it started. He and Beatrice were high school sweethearts all those years ago. They married soon after. It was a church wedding, and Beatrice was beautiful. Life was good. He got a job with the sheriff's department; they bought a house, and everything was heaven on earth.

At least for a time.

Two years into the marriage, Beatrice discovered she was pregnant. C.W. was thrilled. The baby, Jolie Bea Sparkman was born at Winchester General on Feb 4, 1939. She was a gorgeous infant and an even more beautiful toddler. Secretly, Sparky had wanted a boy. What father didn't? But he found the loving, joyful Jolie more than an adequate replacement. It was a good thing, as well. The delivery had mangled Beatrice's womb. There would not be another.

Jolie's death was a blow that the Sparkman family barely lived through. It was an awful time, and Sparkman, who considered himself a God-fearing man, had cursed his god and turned from him, not returning in all these years.

Beatrice had taken it infinitely worse.

Who could blame either of them? Parents should not have to bury their child, their only child.

And he could blame Beatrice. It had been an accident. A horrible, terrible accident. He was sure of it.

Wasn't he?

Now the sheriff had quite a mess on his hands. The murders were one thing. A big thing. But the abductions were another. Ever since the first body had been reported, he'd been mentally constructing a link between the two. Not because they *were* connected but because they *needed to be*. He needed them to be.

Footsteps in the hallway. He looked up to see Beatrice in the doorway, a mug of steaming coffee in her hands. "Sparky?" she said tentatively.

"I'm awake," he assured her.

"What are we going to do?"

"We will handle it. I'll handle all of it."

"I love you," she said."

"I know you do," he replied. "I love you, too."

She sipped her coffee and remained standing, looking in on him.

"You shouldn't be out there at night, you know," he said. Beatrice didn't speak; she merely nodded. "What were you doing?" he asked. Beatrice looked down to the floor and slowly moved over to him. "Are the girls okay? All of them?"

"They are."

"What did you do?"

"Nothing, Sparky, I promise. I just...I just needed to see them."

"Have you made your choice?" he asked. She looked up at him then. Tears welled in the corner of her eyes. Her sorrow was palatable. "No," she mouthed without voice.

Sheriff C.W. Sparkman drained the last bit of whiskey from his glass. He stood up and took his wife into his arms. Beatrice took his hug and embraced him back, mindful of the hot coffee. She laid her head on his shoulder.

After kissing his wife sweetly, he moved away.

"Where are you going?" she asked.

"Back to the station."

"Why?"

"I think I know how to make all this go away."

"Really?" she gasped, excitement evident in her voice.

"Yes, I think so."

Her coffee cup fell to the floor, forgotten. Beatrice almost jumped on her husband, and he had to take several steps back to keep himself from falling. She wasted no time in slobbering kisses all over his face. He laughed, allowed it to continue for a moment, and then pushed her back. "Let's save the celebrating until I get back."

"Then we can be one big happy family, Jolie, you, me."

"Yes, dear," the sheriff said, looking back out the window, this time his eyes falling on the barn. "You, me and Jolie."

21

IT WAS the smallest of sounds, but inside the large, silent room, cool as a tomb and almost as dark, it was easily noticeable. Especially if you were like Mark Borden and on the precipice between slumber and wakefulness. Mark opened his eyes at the sound but remained still. He lay on the bunk, his knees tucked up to his chest to try to stay warm. But, of course, a month or two later in the year, there'd be little issue staying warm. In the Mississippi summer, you could quickly broil alive in a place like this. But, unfortunately, summer was not yet here.

Mark listened closely as a door moved on its hinges. Muffled footsteps entered, and the door swung back on its hinges. It wasn't the same door the deputy brought him through earlier. That one was further away. This one was much closer. He vaguely remembered seeing a back door earlier but thought little of it until now.

The subdued footfalls approached. Mark slowly closed his eyes and began to breathe deeply as if asleep.

For a long moment, nothing happened. It felt as if Mark could feel eyes on him, but he told himself he was being childish. This was a county building that operated day and night. Probably just a deputy taking a shortcut through the building. But if that were true, shouldn't he have heard that same person continue on to the other door?

That brought a chill to Mark's skin.

"You playing possum?" a man whispered. Mark's breath caught in his throat, but he was reasonably confident he didn't show it. He stayed there, eyes closed tight, and his arms wrapped around his legs. He didn't recognize the voice. It had been too low to catch fully.

The next sound was not another whisper, nor was it hushed walking. Instead, it was the sharp jangling of keys. Finally, he heard the slight sound of metal upon metal, and he could no longer just lay there waiting to see what would happen.

Mark Borden opened his eyes to see Sheriff Sparkman step into the cell. In one hand, he held a bed sheet. On the other, his pistol. The gun was trained on Mark.

"Sheriff?" Mark managed in a hoarse voice.

The man moved as if Mark's lips hadn't parted. He entered the cell and threw the sheet down on the bed. He motioned for Mark to stand. "Up," he added, just in case of any confusion. There wasn't. At least on Mark's end. The problem was he didn't move fast enough for the sheriff. "God damn it, I said up."

Mark nodded vigorously. "Okay, okay, Sheriff, I'm a-movin'." And he was. Mark Borden shuffled to his feet, embarrassed to be in his drawers and more than a little shaken about the gun. He hadn't done a thing. He was just lying here. And then he saw that the sheet the sheriff had tossed over to the bed had a noose tied to one end, and his blood ran cold. He knew what the sheriff meant to do.

"Now, grab hold of that sheet and step up on the bed."

"No, sir, no Sheriff. Now, this ain't right." Mark put his hands up. Not in a defensive manner but more of a pleading gesture. The dad-gum man meant to string him up right then and there. Mr. Harper had told him he was rightfully entitled under the law without the benefit of counsel, trial or jury.

"Keep your voice down, boy. Do as you're told."

Still shaking his head, Mark kept trying to reason with the man.

He was ill-equipped for such trying situations, which rankled his nature, but he was no fool. The sheriff had murder in his eyes, and there was little doubt he meant business.

"Sheriff, I didn't do it. I'm innocent. I didn't hurt nobody."

"But you did, you dumb fool. You did. You see, you did it all. You stalked grown men and heartlessly took their lives, robbing their families, loved ones, and friends of decent human beings and snatching away their breadwinners. I'd say you left them in worse shape than you found them. And that's just the start of it, Borden. Yes, it is. Just the start of it."

"I don't understand, sheriff," Mark said but made no move to either step up on the bunk or take hold of the twisted sheet.

"Ain't that a newsflash, bubba." The sheriff laughed then. It was a horrible sound. Grating and icy. "I swear, the best thing your mama could have done for you would have been to take you out back on the day you were born and smash your head against the biggest rock she could find."

Mark didn't like that. He didn't like it one darn bit. He took a step forward. The sheriff matched his move. And for just an instant, he thought the sheriff had changed his mind and decided to shoot him. But the crack that rang through his head wasn't that of a gunshot. Sparkman slapped him. Swung like a big-league pitcher and belted him with an open palm.

Tears instantly stung his eyes, and even the dim room was suddenly too bright.

"Get up on the bed and loop that sheet over the pipe above your head," the sheriff said. Then, still assuming Mark was the mental equivalent of a cucumber, he gestured the action intended with the barrel of his pistol.

"You see, there's been a lot of young girls come up missing. All around here. Hasn't been a suspect in months. Now, we have one."

"I haven't done anything like that, Sheriff. You know that. I didn't kill those men, and I ain't hurt no girls."

"I know no such thing, Mr. Borden. See, the night shift deputy gave me a call. Said you wanted to make a confession. Murdering and kidnapping were weighing heavily on your mind, you said. Well, I came down. You'd already decided you couldn't do the prison time or stand to be locked up at the nuthouse, so you took your sheet, and you took yourself out of the equation, as they say."

"But I didn't confess. All that's a lie."

"It'll be me and my deputy's word against…well, that of a dead man," Sparkman said.

"You might as well shoot me. I ain't stretching my own neck, Sheriff," Mark said in a rare display of bravado. Then the sheriff raised his hand again. The same one he slapped the custodian with. Mark's words might have been brave, but he folded at the implied violence. Instead, he began doing as the sheriff demanded. He was trembling in fear and praying for a miracle. But he did not see this ending, in any way, in his favor. It was all too much for him.

"Are you crying?" the sheriff asked, appalled. Mark avoided looking straight at the sheriff. Instead, he swung the noose end of the sheet around like a cowboy with a lasso and tossed it upward. He missed the pipe by a country mile. "Jesus Christ. You are, aren't ya?" The sheriff shook his head. "Damn it, Borden. I figure I'm doing you a favor, really."

Mark's second attempt failed, although by not such a large margin as before.

"Yeah, seems like your whole life has been a misery. Being born a dummy and all."

The third time was the charm. The knotted end of the sheet flew high and true, dropping on the opposite side of the water pipe.

"Good boy," the sheriff said. "Now, jump down with that other end and tie it around one of these bars."

Mark couldn't think of anything to do but do as he was told. He was deathly afraid of the sheriff.

"Tie it tight, now. We don't want it to let go, do we?" the sheriff chuckled. "Back on the bed, loop it around your neck."

Mark started to speak the sheriff's name, but all he could get out was the hissing sound of a snake. Then he grunted and looked back to the man holding him at gunpoint. The sheriff was looking at him, but his eyes looked off to the side, almost like the man himself couldn't look his victim in the eye.

And then the sheriff met his eyes, and the lack of emotion took Mark's breath. The man did not care. He was not torn by his actions. He had no second thoughts. This was a task to be completed and nothing besides.

Mark took a big step without a choice and was again standing on his jailhouse bunk.

"Say your prayers, Borden. Maybe Jesus will have mercy on your pitiful soul." With that, Sheriff C.W. Sparkman flicked the business end of his gun at Mark one last time.

Mark Borden, who'd never asked a thing from this life but to be left alone, perhaps fit in, swallowed hard and placed his neck in the sheet. "Pull it tight," the sheriff said. He did.

"All right, Mark, all you have to do is walk. One step. Do it?"

Mark didn't. He couldn't. Facing death in seconds, he no longer cared that the sheriff had brandished a sidearm. But now that the sheriff had him right where he wanted him, he did not need Borden's cooperation. Sparkman moved faster than Mark had thought possible. He grabbed Mark's bare leg and yanked. Despite his efforts to evade the sheriff's grasp, there was nowhere to go and nothing to hold to. Mark lost his footing.

And he slipped from the bed. The sheet snapped tautly, and Mark swung eight inches over the floor and started to flail his arms and legs.

At that moment, the back door burst open.

22

TOM HARPER just couldn't get tonight out of his mind. He'd gone home and climbed out of the car, his back aching and his eyes burning from lack of sleep

He'd never seen Sparky so riled up with a suspect. Sure, these killings were atrocious, and the pressure had to get to him, but Tom wasn't convinced Borden was their guy. Yes, he'd brought him in, just as he'd do with anyone walking dark roads at night covered in blood that wasn't their own and unable to account for the last few hours.

Then again, Mark Borden was a unique soul, wasn't he? Did that mean he couldn't have been the killer? Of course not. Tom was a patrol supervisor and didn't often get involved with investigations, but he had a natural knack for these things. And like the history lesson from Willie Truitt, maybe the dummy had been the killer, or maybe not. History did not let go of its secrets so easily.

But tonight, with the sheriff's anger up, he seemed more capable of murder than Mark Borden.

Tom needed sleep. A lot of it. He needed to lay down, drift away, regain his strength, and get his mind to whirring again. It was as if his mental gears were stuck in cold molasses, and his eyes were filled with a bushel of sand.

But instead, he got back up off the bed, took just a few minutes to brew half a pot of coffee and headed back to the car. This time he climbed in his highway patrol cruiser.

There was something about the sheriff's actions that he just couldn't justify.

The drive was inconsequential. He didn't so much as pass another car. But when he pulled to the back of the sheriff's department, he saw the sheriff's own cruiser parked in the back.

They had left together. Sparkman had apparently returned.

But why?

Lieutenant Tom Harper got a horrible feeling and decided to act on it. He parked just behind the sheriff's car. There was space for him to park, but he didn't use those. He had that sick feeling he was about to catch a dear old friend of his in the act of something. He wasn't sure what, but he would soon find out.

He didn't pull his sidearm as he opened the door, but once he stepped in, he wished he had.

At first, he couldn't discern the scene unfolding before him. Then, reflexively, he took a step back and gasped.

Mark Borden was hanging from the ceiling, a dingy yellow sheet wrapped around his neck. Instead of trying to cut him down, Sparkman held a gun on him, and…hell, it looked like he was intent on the man dying right in front of him.

Mark's body flailed as he tried to catch the tip of his toes back on top of the bunk. He was like a man drowning only feet from the riverbank. He struggled and fought, but Sparkman swatted his legs out from under him each time he got close. His hands kept fighting and fidgeting at his neck to loosen the sheet enough to breathe. Finally, as his face turned blue, it was apparent he was failing.

"Sheriff," Tom Harper hollered, his hand already going for his weapon.

C.W. was at an advantage. His gun was already drawn. The

sheriff pivoted to the right. Then, instinctually, his finger squeezed the trigger.

THE GUNSHOT WAS LIKE THUNDER IN THE ENCLOSED AREA, AND Mark's body went straight as a board. And for half a heartbeat, his body went still. Sparkman looked back at him. He found Mark motionless and quiet. He began to smile. The door to the front of the station burst open, and Deputy Settlemires looked like he'd just woken up. He wasn't ready for the sights he took in. A man crumpled on the floor next to the back door. The sheriff standing there, smoke billowing from the muzzle of his pistol and the jail's sole evening resident hanging suspended from the ceiling.

Settlemires had received a call from the sheriff earlier. Told him that no matter what, he was not to come into the jail section tonight. Settlemires hadn't shared he had no intentions of checking on Borden and was planning to catch up on missed sleep. But when the sheriff sweetened the pot with the promise of a promotion to sergeant, Settlemires had fallen asleep thinking of the extra money he'd start earning in his monthly pay. But the gunshot had startled him awake, and while he wasn't sure what he'd find, this apparently wasn't it.

No one seemed to notice Mark's right hand. His arm was ramrod straight down at his side, just like the other. His fingers splayed open, then curled closed as if holding a baseball bat. Then the fingers flicked out once more.

The sheriff turned to Settlemires, who already had his hands up. He was shaking his head for Sparkman not to shoot.

Sparkman cursed under his breath and turned back to Mark Borden.

But there was no longer a Mark Borden to look at. In the blink of an eye, the sheriff noticed several things about the man. He was no longer slack, he was no longer panicked, and he was looking right at Sparkman with the most awful yellow eyes. Across his lips rested the most satisfied sneer.

"What in the hell," the sheriff said, blinking his eyes, apparently momentarily forgetting the gun in his hand.

DARK OPENED HIS EYES JUST IN TIME.

Death by hanging is rarely what most people believe. Most assume the neck is broken and the hanging victim dies instantly by way of a hangman's fracture. This decidedly nasty colloquial term refers to fracturing the vertebra in the neck. In fact, a hauntingly low number of deaths are committed this way. It mostly occludes the blood vessels more often than asphyxiation awaiting those on the rope's end. Which is not instant and can last minutes, all while the victim is in pure, unadulterated agony. That is the very reason sentences of hanging announced in antiquarian courts often included the line, "*and hang by the neck until dead.*"

In Dark's case, while Mark had not broken his neck and he was a minute or so away from death, serious injury can result in the suspension of a human body by the neck at any time on the way to kicking the bucket. If Mark had been paralyzed... Well, he hadn't. And now, he was out of danger.

Dark grunted and jerked once. The taut sheet tore. Bending his knees slightly on impact, Dark landed nimbly on his feet. He pinched the remaining material around his neck between his thumb and forefinger and tossed it behind him.

To the sheriff, he said, "Don't worry about hell, sheriff. I'll make sure to tune you up before you get there." Then, in that darkened space, in a little old jail cell in the middle of Nowhere, Dixie, something else happened.

Arcs of silver electricity ignited. The bolts were thin, wire-like. They had ignited at the fingertips, quickly enveloped the hand, and then rode the air above his flesh up his arms.

Realizing he was now not only at a physical advantage over the other men but was now leaps or bounds beyond them, he grinned and said, "Ooh, there it is."

Before the deputy still standing in the open door or Sparkman could react, Dark slapped his hands together, and the lone lamp's bulb burst, plunging them all into darkness. The subtle glow of the currents surrounding Dark was inconsequential but put on a rather spectacular light show in the enclosed area.

A muzzle flash from the sheriff's pistol spat and lit the nearest wall in a moving shadow. Bullets struck the cinder block walls, showering invisible shrapnel all about.

Then the sheriff screamed as Dark's hand tightened around his neck. He'd stepped behind the sheriff so gracefully that Sparky hadn't noticed. Now it was too late.

"Oh yeah, they'll love you down there, Sheriff. You got a set of lungs made for screaming." Dark took immense satisfaction as he pounded the man's head against the wall until there was no more thud on impact, just a sickly plopping sound. Then, he allowed the body to drop to the ground. "That was over before it got good and started," he said and then laughed.

He turned and found the open doorway was empty. It led to a dark corridor. The sorry-ass deputy had skipped town, it seemed.

The aura of energy surrounding him faded away.

It took Dark less than two minutes to locate the cardboard box his clothing and possessions had been hastily stowed earlier in the evening. Up front, the station was quiet. Dark slipped into the robe and tossed his murder tools into the pockets. He turned and walked back into the jail area. He passed Tom Harper on his way out. The man wasn't dead but in a world of pain. His pant leg was soaked in blood.

"You know, if I had just taken care of you earlier, none of this would have been necessary."

"Help me," Harper pleaded, barely able to string the words together. Perspiration coated his face, but he looked like a tough old bird.

"But rules are rules, and you're not mine to kill," Dark said as he passed him by, paying no mind to his begging. "But I must admit, it's been fun."

23

"COME ALONG, JOLIE," Mother said. "A lady doesn't dawdle." The three girls did as they were told. Kathryn led the trio. As for now, she felt like she was Mother's favorite. That meant something. Right now, it meant everything she knew.

Behind her was Melia. She was holding together okay, but Kathryn could tell she wasn't far from acting an awful lot like Wendy.

They'd all been woken by Mother's entrance into the barn. For a brief time, Kathryn had fallen into a dreamless sleep that was the best she'd had since getting grabbed at the edge of her driveway all those days ago. She'd come in barking at the girls with all the veracity of a Doberman.

"Up and at 'em, girls. We have little time to waste. Come, come, tea is on," she shouted at what had to be the top of her lungs.

It was still dark outside, and the air was cool. It took an effort for Kathryn to get to her feet, and she took the time it took the other two to rise to shake her slumber from her head.

The chilly air helped wake the young girls as they crossed the lawn from the barn to the house. Kathryn saw whatever car had pulled up earlier was gone as they stepped up into the house.

Mother waited for all three to file in and closed the door behind them. Kathryn heard her engage the lock and felt her heart slip further into her gut.

Mother led them into the changing room. Wendy had required the most help getting dressed. Kathryn had tried to help them both, and she tried to do a good job. She hated she'd done that now. She should have been smarter. Messed up something about their dress, shoes, or hair. Something that would make them less than the ideal Jolie.

She didn't want them to die, but she wanted to live.

But it was too late for that. Mother was back and herding them out of the changing room. Their dresses weren't identical, but they were close enough in appearance that a casual onlooker would say they were. The clothes were a pretty light blue, like a robin's egg. It was a striking spring color. But nothing about them looked pretty or fresh.

Even to Kathryn's eyes, all three of them looked quite pitiable.

They traveled a short, dark corridor from the changing room to another door. This one didn't close like other doors but swung both in and out. Mother pushed it in to reveal a moderately sized dining room. There were place settings for two only. Which was not out of the ordinary but having them all here at the same time was.

"Here we are, girls," Mother said. "Things will be different tonight." None of the girls spoke. Instead, they stood there, their hands clasped together in front of them at their waists and their faces pointed to their feet.

"I've missed my Jolie for a long time. A very long time. And now it's time to have her back. But, as I said, there can be only one. And tonight, we decide which one of you it will be."

Kathryn looked at her sharply. She wasn't being coy about it anymore. Instead, she was being open and honest, so Kathryn, somehow, mustered up the courage to ask the question she was afraid she already knew the answer to.

"What happens to the two of us you don't choose?" The girl's voice was fragile. She was terrified, but she took some advice from her father, who always put on a brave face for the world. Kathryn stood tall, with her shoulders wide. She looked up at the taller woman with clear eyes, and her chin protruded.

Mother didn't answer straight away. Instead, she looked down at Kathryn, and the little girl wilted beneath the stare.

"Curiosity killed the cat, little one," she said. Kathryn felt she'd committed a grave atrocity by expressing her concerns. The moment stretched on. Kathryn's mouth went dry like the desert during a heat wave.

Mother, who'd moved to the table and stood behind a chair, her hands resting upon the chairback, swooped over to the girls as if her feet didn't even need the benefit of the floor beneath them.

Kathryn's first instinct was to shrink back behind the others. But at the last possible moment, she willed herself sentinel. She stood there, her father's daughter.

Mother touched her shoulder with the tips of her fingers, urging her toward another door she'd never seen the other side of. Kathryn's feet moved in the direction she was urged. Behind her, both Melia and Wendy followed. Mother pushed open the door, and they were in another part of the house. Dark, with only the most subtle lighting, Kathryn had to follow Mother closely. She looked around, but the shadows hid most of the room.

"Eyes forward," Mother said as she noticed Kathryn and Melia looking around. "Mind your step," she said as they approached several steps leading down into what looked like a den. It was lit brighter by a set of twin floor lamps.

The room looked normal. That was extraordinary on its own to Kathryn. There were bookshelves crammed with hardcovers. A colorful rug was in front of a television set made into a wooden cabinet, with knick-knacks spread across the top. Like in her grandma's house, doilies sat on the end tables and a coffee table in front of a sofa.

Kathryn had imagined much more dreadful and shocking décor. Like body parts hung in place of framed photographs, decanters of blood sitting about, and perhaps even a rug made out of human flesh in place of the bright carpeting.

At the far end of the room, there was yet another door. This one looked heavier, with a window covering the top half. Curtains concealed what lay on the other side, but Kathryn guessed it was another exterior door.

In a flash of motion, Mother spun around, stepped past Kathryn, then past Melia, and grabbed Wendy harshly by her chin. Then, with her thumb and fingers, she squeezed tightly. "Why are you whining, little girl?" Mother demanded.

Kathryn was shocked. She hadn't even heard the girl make a sound. But she was busy checking out their surroundings. But, knowing Wendy, she was probably making some sad sound or perhaps sobbing.

"She's scared," Kathryn said. She tried to be brave, but her voice quivered. Mother rounded on her then, but Kathryn stood firm.

"What did you say, missy?"

Kathryn swallowed hard. "I said she's scared. Like we all are. How could we not be? You take us from our homes, put us in cages, make us dress up in these old musty dresses and pretend to be someone we're not."

If rage was a mask, Kathryn would have said Mother pulled it on. Instead, her eyes widened, and her face became grim, her lips parting to bare her teeth. She studied Kathryn in silence, and the young girl quivered all inside. But as hard as it was, she never dropped her eyes from Mother's.

Finally, Mother spoke. "I've treated you all very well. But, my patience, kind as it may be, has worn thin. If you were scared before," she said, snatching Kathryn by her collar and leaning down to her face. "Wait until you see real fear."

DARK SHOT DOWN THE STREET IN TOM HARPER'S HIGHWAY PATROL CAR. It was a big beefy 1955 Buick Century with a powerful V8 under the hood. This wasn't the usual car ordered by the state of Mississippi but was more prevalent out west in states like California and issued only to specially designated supervisors with the rank of lieutenant or above.

The bubblegum light whirled. The rotating light sliced through the dark night, only outshone by the headlights.

With the speedometer needle still climbing, the motor growled monstrously beneath the hood, accompanied by the building feline whine of fuel feeding it. Behind the wheel–which needed a surprising amount of correction—Dark cackled like the maniac he was.

The state police car sped down the city streets from the sheriff's department, awakening those living nearby from a deep sleep. While Dark had never driven an automobile, he took readily to the task, understanding the mechanisms and applications as he needed them. The keys had been in the ignition, and as the engine sparked to life, he was already dropping the car into reverse while he slipped the parking brake.

He knew exactly where he was going. He knew exactly how to get there. But he had to hurry. This time, he was being allowed to intercede before the worst of the violence against an innocent struck.

Instead of anxiety or worry, Mr. Dark and Scary gleefully steered the big car through the streets of Farmington with wind from the open windows blowing through his hair and across his face. His laughter rolled out into the night, lost beneath the Buick's labors.

As the Buick shot past the drive-in on the far side of town, where the late show ended hours ago, two teenagers, Brian White and Tim Wool were picking up the last of the trash from the parking lot.

"Jesus Christ, boy, look at that thing fly," Brian said. Tim stood a few feet away and was doing his best to keep his eyes open said, "What's that?" but caught sight of the incredibly bright blue light and the speed as it approached. The rumble of the engine reached his ears less than a second later. The two stood there and watched it zoom closer, and then it was there, and in the same instant, they watched the taillights shrink down in the distance.

"That was Old Man Harper, wasn't it?" Tim asked.

"Looked like him," Brian agreed.

Breezing through the residential area into the rural farmland, Dark pressed the pedal to the floor and held it there.

"Fuck me," Dark took a moment to say, "I have been missing out." Then, looking down at the dash, he noticed the car radio above the police band. Not giving a damn what other cops might be talking about, he twisted the chrome knob nearest him. Bill Hailey and His Comets filled the cabin of the cruiser, rocking out to "Shake, Rattle and Roll."

Sheriff Sparkman and his wife owned a large parcel of land several miles out of town. It was a nice spread that the old lawdog couldn't have afforded on his salary alone. It was the wife who came from money—old money. Oldest money in town, actually. It was easily five miles out to the Sparkman property, and after the drive-in theater, there was little more than open road and a few farms back off the road in between. The Buick was soaring now.

Blue-lit landscapes flew by in a blur, and the Buick jumped and thrashed like a wild bull. For his part, Dark held onto the steering wheel like a cowboy in a rodeo. He laughed, he shouted, and he sang along with the radio.

Gravel flew high, and clouds of dust billowed behind as the car careened onto the long gravel driveway leading up to the house. The tail end of the big car smacked the mailbox along the back right panel, but Dark wasn't bothered. Instead, he pressed the accelerator again and shot up the drive.

Within seconds he braked hard in the lawn, rutting up twin tufts of grass and soil. Then he was up and out of the car, his hands pulling both weapons from his robe.

"Lucy, I'm home," Dark called.

24

MOTHER STOOD THERE, watching as the three girls took in the contents of the chest freezers. She hated to admit it, but she enjoyed watching their faces change from terrified little sniveling brats to fully understanding their fates for displeasing her. It was the ultimate power, like being a parent and mother. The power of life or death was the most intoxicating thing she'd ever felt in all her life. It was the only thing that filled her since Jolie's death. It was the only thing that ever could.

Until she had her Jolie back, that was.

The freezers were each placed against the wall inside the garage. The salesman in the Sears up in Tupelo had told her and Sparky the 1955 Coldspot freezers held twenty cubic feet of frozen meals. With eleven convenient storage sections, the Coldspot could store up to 350 meals and was the best-selling deep freezer for three years. So, they'd bought two of them. Had them delivered the next day.

Beatrice was confident the young salesman with the slicked-back hair had never considered his wares would be used in such an unintended fashion.

Inside each, young, precious children lay. But unfortunately, these girls couldn't toe the line in Beatrice's search for a suitable replacement for her beloved daughter. Instead, their flesh was tinged with blue and ice crystals had formed in their hair, eyebrows, and eyelashes.

"This is what happens when you don't do as you are told, children," Mother warned. "You never see your folks again. You never again feel their loving touch. They will lay awake the rest of their lives wondering what became of you. It will haunt them, I'm sure. All the while, you lay in the darkness, young and beautiful and alone forever." And then, considering, she added, "Or until we find a good place to bury your bones."

The trio of little girls said nothing. Instead, they stood there in their dresses, looking at the freezer in front of them. They all looked as if they were about to lose their minds. That made Mother smile.

That smile faltered as the sound of a racing car engine reached her ears. Mother twirled toward the closed garage door, and the sound grew louder and louder still. Then, finally, she stepped closer and saw headlights splash across the garage windows.

"Girls, back in the house. Hurry, hurry," Mother called. Only the girls, this time, didn't respond. Mother was not used to her orders being dismissed so thoroughly. As a matter of fact, she was halfway to the door leading into the house before she realized the girls weren't at her heels.

Her voice thundered within the confines of the garage. Mother was the epitome of the proper southern lady or was the façade she adopted. When it slipped away, there was hell to pay.

Kathryn knew the signs and braced for the fit. But the car engine grew louder, and then there was a great commotion, and the motor sound died away and was replaced by the slam of a car door.

Silence fell heavy inside.

Something from the outside hammered a fist against the garage door. The heavy wooden door trembled in its tracks. It sounded like sharp thunder, and the girls whooped and hollered, Wendy, being the loudest of them all. "Quiet, damn it," Mother spat.

Mother, dressed as she was in her evening gown and heels,

pearls strung around her neck, with a powdered face but her hair tight in rollers, was quite a sight. Yet, when she twisted on herself, something akin to worry for the first time burrowed quick and shallow crevices through her cheeks.

Kathryn almost felt like smiling.

She almost screamed out for help, but something in Mother's eyes caught her attention and stayed her tongue.

"Sparky?" she called. "Chris? Christopher William, is that you?" Mother's voice was calm, even gentle. Not the fake, put-on voice she'd used on the girls. This one was gentle, almost normal. Nothing nor no one answered her.

Instead, whoever was on the outside was attempting to raise the long and wide wooden door that worked by way of a balance rod that pivoted the door from closed and opened and in its open state, the rod supported the door while it was open. Simple and effective. But the small dark gap at the bottom where the door met cement only raised a few inches and then stopped.

"Come on, girls. Move it now, or I swear to God I'll—" while she'd not been speaking loudly but more an angry half-whisper, a voice tunneled through the night and the sturdy walls that separated the four of them from the free, outside world.

"You'll not lay a finger more on those girls, woman."

The voice gave Kathryn the chills, but she was delighted as they rode like sharks splitting the sea. They covered her arms and legs because she was looking right at Mother. The crevices of worry had deepened to ravines, and her eyes grew wide, and she stepped backward toward the door.

But she quickly turned her attention back to the girls. This time she did whisper, but her words bore no less veracity at the lower volume. "Go. Inside." The words had the slick feel of a serpent's hiss. There was no time.

There was a horrendous twisting of metal that overpowered everything inside the garage. The sound drove a spike of pure ice into the girls' hearts. Beatrice, for her part, felt a chill of terror prickle her spine.

The ground beneath them, solid concrete, trembled underfoot. Some incredible force tore the large door from its facing. Beatrice watched as it was tossed to the side, careening through the lawn to reveal the visitor. Car lights shone from behind a large man, draped in a flowing blackness, bathing the garage in both light and shadow.

Beatrice craned her neck as far as she could to see the man's face. The way the headlights rolled over his substantial form, and at this angle, almost blinded them all. But she did see something. Something totally unexpected.

The eyes of madness peered at her through the distance. Eyes of awful amber, of sickness, of pestilence.

"Word is, somebody's been misbehavin'," the stranger said in a deep voice that sounded like it was on the verge of laughter. Insane laughter. He took a slow step forward.

Then another.

FOR A MOMENT, THE WOMAN SAID NOTHING. DARK SCANNED THE inside of the room. A large garage with no car. Two massive, long electric freezers against the side wall. A door on the wall adjacent to it. The sheriff's wife and three little girls. They looked as terrified as any he'd ever seen.

"Who are you? This is private property," the woman said, but without conviction.

Dark pointed, "Trespassing or kidnapping, which do you think is worse?"

"Do you know who I am? You're messing in business that doesn't concern you. And you'll pay the price for it."

Dark stepped further into the garage. His yellow eyes stayed on Mother. His robe flowed with his movement. He crackled the knuckles of one hand and then the other. Silver energy sparkled from them. "I rightfully don't give a damn who you are." Dark looked her over quickly from head to toe and gave her an exaggerated wink. "Cute, get up, doll. Nice makeup job. But I'm a firm believer in the saying, you can polish a turd, but it's still just a turd."

The girls shrank back, almost in unison. It was as if this strange newcomer talking in such a manner to Mother was almost more unbelievable than him wrenching away the wide door of the garage.

Dark eased forward.

"Stop where you are, stranger," Beatrice Sparkman commanded.

"Hmm, if it's all the same to you, I'd rather not." Dark did slow his already measured tread and turned to Kathryn as she seemed to be the one holding up best. "Lead them out. Find help," he said almost compassionately.

The girl did not do as he said. Instead, she hazarded a glance back at the woman.

"Did you not hear me, child," Dark admonished sharply. The silver electricity accentuated his eyes for a second, making him seem even more demonically deranged.

It was the girl at the end. She was the one that appeared to be walking while catatonic, which took Dark's words to heart. She turned from the others and started sprinting.

The woman was quick. Dark had to give her that. But he, of course, was quicker. With no desire to injure the girls, despite how close he was to his target, he slung down both hands simultaneously. A bluish-tinted white light ate up the darkness like a hungry beast in a mere instant. The light was enough to distract Beatrice but not enough to keep the much younger girls from jumping their asses into gear and running after the other.

When the light died away, Mother started to pursue.

"Naw, I don't think so. Besides, there's a trail that will lead right back to you anyhow. Probably by morning." That stopped Beatrice as she considered the implications of his words. It took her a moment, one that Dark gave her freely. It sweetened the taste, he found.

"Sparky?" Mother asked. Her face changed. She might have been scared of Mr. Dark and Scary, but she no longer showed it. Instead, something looked to have collapsed in her face, as if gravity pulled just a little harder at her flesh.

"I see you're quicker than most blondes. He's no longer with us, I'm afraid, doll." It was as if his words had teeth biting into her tender flesh. She had questions, he saw but knew this wasn't the time or place for them, just as she probably figured he wasn't a fellow to be asking such questions. "He won't be darkening your door anymore."

"You bastard," Mother said. Her voice was a low, rumbling shot of anger, but again, Dark didn't care. In fact, he reveled in it.

Dark took a good look around. His eyes settled on the large white appliances behind the woman along the far wall. He knew their contents as soon as he focused his cold yellow eyes on them.

The contents, the state of the little, frail corpses within, and the hell they endured at the hands of this filthy wench. Theirs was a suffering unearned, yet one they had paid heftily for. Each of them. Five young souls, taken by a raving lunatic and aided by her spine-less husband.

He saw their time here. Locked in pens not suited for pigs. He could taste their fear. But, unlike that of his victims, it was a sour mash. He felt as if they felt as, one by one, snuffed out like a candle's flame. Sometimes painfully, sometimes mercifully. But at all times, final.

"I'm no softy, you dirty cunt, but I don't much go for folk that kidnap, torture, mutilate and kill little girls. So in that way, I may also be a bit old-fashioned."

"You, you don't understand. You can't understand."

"I think I just pretty much said that myself. But of course, you're special. You're different. You're just snatching kids off the street, putting them through your psychotic little game. And if they don't fill the hole, you fucking dug out by yourself by being a piece of cowshit, momma, you just," Dark snapped his fingers, and the sound was loud and sharp, 'start over? Is that it?"

"What did you say?" The woman almost forgot her situation and charged at Dark. But she did not.

"I know all about your daughter. Why is Jolie dead? Why is she not here instead of these poor kids? Tell me, Beatrice, what happened?"

That started a chain reaction deep inside Beatrice Sparkman. "Go to hell, you bastard. It was an accident. Nothing but a tragic accident."

"Whatever you have to tell yourself so you can sleep at night."

"Shut up!" Beatrice shouted. "Shut up, damn you!"

Dark grinned. He was getting under her skin. "I don't think I will. Tell me, Beatrice, or do you prefer I call you Mother? Tell me about little Jolie."

"Somehow, you already know, don't you," Beatrice said.

"Do I know that you held a pillow over her face until she smothered to death?"

"Shut your mouth, you dirty bastard."

Dark moved closer. He swept the sides of his robe back and peered at Beatrice.

Something struck him as a bit peculiar. She was angry. Yes, she was a woman, so that was expected. But Dark could sense very little fear from her. That was unexpected. Was he losing his touch?

"What do you say, let this old feller here take you for a twirl."

"You're imbued," the woman said. She spoke it strangely, almost brazenly.

"Pardon?" Dark had been thrown by that.

"You're nothing special, buster. You're just another specter born from the dirt of Winchester."

"Say again?" Dark said. But like everything, he knew it as she said, not a moment before. He had not doubted who he was, why he was. He was here, a spirit of vengeance, a specter of revenge. That was all that mattered. Or so he had thought.

"Surely, you know."

'What's to know?"

Something akin to merriment danced in Beatrice's eyes. She didn't have to say his word. In his mind, the power that propelled him was revealed wholly and completely: Winchester County is cursed, the very land. Or blessed, depending on your point of view. When man's actions become too evil, threatening the land's peace, he now stood acts. It has a certain power it can use to tip the scales back in its favor. That's Winchester, the real Winchester. And that was all he knew. That and for some dark deal sealed in secret never shared to prosperity, nothing that Winchester can throw at the world can harm anyone human being with the blood of Roland Winchester in their veins. The way Dark looked at it, he was pretty much screwed.

But what the hell, it was the most action he'd seen in a long time.

Dark's yellow eyes narrowed, and his eyelids were slits. "Enough of this."

Dark moved in for the attack.

25

DARK SPREAD his arms shoulder-width in front of him. Between his palms, silver currents arced. The force built as he watched the widow Sparkman's reaction.

It was not what he expected. Beatrice watched with interest but didn't shy away from the supernatural power on display.

"This is going to hurt you a lot more than me, I'm afraid. But I promise I won't make you suffer too long," Dark said. He took one step back with his left leg and, bracing himself, shot great waves of energy straight at her. There would be nothing left of her or her clothing, he knew.

Or thought he knew.

Inches from her body, the energy split decisively as Moses parted the Red Sea. Then, the energy splashed harmlessly to her side, curving away from its intended target.

"What in the hell," Dark muttered, not believing what he saw.

It was Beatrice Sparkman's turn to smile. But Dark was resourceful if nothing else. Both of his hands disappeared within the robe. They each held a World War I trench knife when they next showed.

Dark lunged at her with the knife in his right hand, the sharp, double-edged dagger, a menacing weapon. He was aiming for her shoulder. He never made it. He was inches from her when he felt something like an electrical bolt zapping his insides. He cried out. One knife, then the other fell to the concrete floor and skidded away.

He wasn't finished with her yet. But he didn't understand what was happening to him. So even as it was happening, the bite of excruciating pain filling him, he took another step toward her.

Then she did something unexpected. She held out her hand, and suddenly Dark was up off his feet, flying like a rag doll. When his back struck the wall, he would have crumpled to the ground if not for the invisible force holding him in place.

"W-What?" he muttered to himself.

"Speak up, man. I can't hear you," Beatrice Sparkman said. There was something different about her. There was steel in her voice.

Dark looked at her. She approached him confidently, her head held high.

"What sort of sorcery is this?" he managed. To Dark, it felt like a thousand pounds of transparent weight were pressing down on him.

"Blood. The best kind, you idiot. I'm more than the wife of a county sheriff. I am a Winchester. Descended from the man himself. And as you seem to know about everything else, don't you know that nothing empowered by the land can harm a Winchester? It's practically carved in stone."

Dark didn't speak. As she spoke the words into existence, he knew them to be true. Hell of a way for things to work. He thought it would have been nice to know this bullshit a few minutes ago. Then again, the laws of nature revealed themselves only as they wished.

The county was founded in 1836 by Roland Winchester. Under mysterious circumstances. So much is yet to be known about that time. However, one thing was and still is certain, the Winchester bloodline remained impervious to the powers of the land itself, and the mystical creatures and demons pulled through from other planes and dimensions using its sacred and profane properties.

And in such times as something mystical did try to harm any of the Winchester bloodlines, they would be able to defend themselves.

It was a law of nature, not of man. It could not be broken. Thankfully, it wasn't the sole rule.

Dark's bones began to crack under the weight of Beatrice Sparkman's power. He'd hate to see what she could do if she were the daughter of Winchester. As it was, the blood had been diluted through the years, but it seemed to be more than sufficient to deal with Dark.

The pressure against him was intense. Dark felt his body crushing slowly through the wall. It was painful, but that was not his consideration at the moment.

She was gaining confidence with each passing moment. And why should she not be encouraged by slapping a man like Dark against the wall and holding him as if he were the runt of a kitten litter, with him being unable to do a thing to stop her, all without breaking a sweat?

"Now," Dark said, though his voice was hoarse and weak, "I wouldn't go and get all cocky, sweetcakes."

It was Mother's turn to laugh now. "You're getting on my last nerve, shadow man. I am a Winchester by birth. I could care less wherever you came from, whoever conjured you up. And I certainly don't care to hear your suggestions."

"That may well be true, you stinking cunt." His voice was almost gone now. The truth was, he didn't have to say a thing. But he would be gone soon, and he thought he might as well have a little fun with it. "But you forget something."

"I forget nothing, ghoul."

His throat was almost closed shut. The invisible force Mrs. Sparkman wielded was an incredible power. One he wished he possessed.

His nose cracked across the bridge, and the floating bone's sharp edges pressed deep into him. A dark, slimy fluid leaked from the corners of his eyes and black goo trickled out over his lips. His ribs fractured, bending as far as they could manage, yet still, he had to say his piece.

"The only Winchester spirit that can kill a Winchester—" that's all Dark could manage. But it was enough.

Beatrice Sparkman looked as if she'd seen a ghost or realized one had been in the garage for several minutes. She went instantly pale. And she finished his words for him. "Is a soul killed by a Winchester."

There was still something burning in Dark. Something deep down still churned with all the biting vengeance and blazing anger that had empowered Dark in this incarnation and all the others.

Mr. Dark and Scary had walked this world many times before and would do so countless times again, but not before sending this bitch straight to Hell.

Silver arcs of electricity crackled across Dark's body, and Beatrice Sparkman, the great-great-granddaughter of Roland Winchester, suddenly understood. Holding one arm out toward Dark, she turned quickly to the two freezers just as twin bolts of zinging electricity shot across the darkness straight into the large metal appliances.

As each bolt slammed into its target, there was a small explosion. Then those same arcs of silver energy quickly enveloped the freezers.

The heavy freezers started to tremble and tremor. They began jumping centimeters off the ground, and then they both crashed, one after the other, back to the ground. Finally, the electricity dissipated, and silence replaced the brief calamity.

After a few moments of pregnant silence, Beatrice looked back at Dark, still suspended against the wall, his life force slowly ebbing away.

"Looks like you blew your load, friend," Beatrice said and then jumped and let loose a scream when the first freezer lid crashed open, broke its hinges, and slapped itself on its side.

Dark, despite the pain, grinned.

"Maybe I can't touch you," he managed between gritted teeth. "But they can."

"No," she whispered as a hand shot up out of the freezer. Dark was all but forgotten as tiny fingers grabbed the side of the makeshift casket. A small child, a young girl, slowly pulled herself from her icy grave. Beatrice stepped back, and not one but two girls-both spookily similar in appearance, from the color of their hair down to the dresses they wore, save for the conditions of their bodies, rose.

The dead girls did not attack immediately. Instead, they waited for their sisters to rise from the matching dark, freezing coffin.

Dark had collapsed to the floor when the girls began to rise, frightening Beatrice and derailing her train of thought. He could move now, but only a little. Being skewered by an energy beam wasn't his idea of a good time; it had taken an awful lot out of him. For now, he remained still, sitting on his rear end, back to the wall. He watched in both fascination and satisfaction as the scene unfolded before him.

Beatrice moved as if her feet were encased in cement. She was mesmerized by the macabre scene unfolding before her. And even Dark had to admit; it was something to see.

There were five of them, all told, when the resurrection was complete. Five once beautiful children now only ghastly semblances of their former selves. Angry red slashes against blue skin. One eyeball popped out, dangling from its socket. Their faces, delicate and tender in life, were hard and jagged in death. Frozen flesh hung slack across cheekbones too sharp. Old, rusty stains spattered their dresses.

"No," Beatrice said. The word lingered on until the silence of the place ate it up. The girls said nothing. They only stood, looking at the woman that had ruined their lives and eventually ended it, leaving their respective families to wonder about the fate of their children.

And then, as if with one mind, they attacked. How such diminutive forms morphed into aggressive attackers was a mystery for the ages. But they did. Their resurrected forms held more power than in a living state, and Dark ensured that. Before, they had been unwilling victims to a stronger woman. Now the roles had been reversed, and the tables turned.

The five surrounded Beatrice Sparkman, who'd gone through just about every facial expression one could imagine but had remained remarkably quiet as they approached, and then the first tiny hand, outstretched, clawed down her back. That got a shrill scream out of the old girl, enough to wake the dead if they weren't already awake.

Soon, the girls toppled the taller woman, but they were not finished. Not finished by a country mile. Each one of the reanimated children, vicious and snarling, did their worst to Beatrice. And each tried to outdo the other. They writhed atop Beatrice. The woman reached out, clawing the air for assistance, for salvation, but no one around was interested in helping her. Just the opposite.

"Help," she said between two huge gulps of air.

One of them tore her jugular, and dark blood sprayed high. Mrs. Sparkman screamed, but it died a quick death, and the only sound was tearing and scraping of flesh and a sad, dying gurgle.

In moments, there was nothing left of Beatrice Sparkman but a ruined mess.

The five girls stopped as if synchronized. Then, they each stood and looked toward Dark. He nodded.

"Sorry, I would have been here sooner if I could've. Just wasn't in the cards." This he spoke without his usual dash of sarcasm.

They each stood there, wearing the faces of monsters. Mr. Dark and Scary knew they were somewhere else now, somewhere better.

Finally satisfied, the girls returned to the freezers and climbed in.

Dark couldn't stand to see them return to their temporary

graves, so he turned without a last glance at Beatrice and left the garage.

Outside, the night sky was brightening in the east, and the stars were fading from sight. Yet, all was quiet and calm.

As he walked, Dark's hand twitched, and the burning yellow in his eyes blazed out. Soon, Mark Borden was wondering just where in the hell he was.

26

MARK TOOK the man-sized door out of the garage and saw the highway patrol car. Off to the side lay a crumpled garage door. That didn't help him understand just how in the world he got here. He tried to remember the last thing he could recall, but it was a blur. First, he was in the cell, trying to sleep, shivering, almost naked on his bunk. Now, he was in what looked like the middle of nowhere, at a house he'd never seen before.

He looked down and saw he was in the blasted black robe once more. Oh, how he hated the thing. He had no idea how he continued to drape himself in it when he blacked out. He hadn't had it in lockup at the sheriff's office. They'd stripped him out of it.

Before he could think about it anymore, headlights appeared. They were zooming up the driveway right toward Mark, a fair distance away. But coming closer. The driveway was gravel, and the sound of the tires crunching over it arrived at his ears moments before the engine growl. The car slid to a halt a dozen yards from him.

Mark stopped walking. He swallowed and gave a little wave to the car. He felt like a moron, but he thought showing manners might help his situation.

The car door opened, and a woman he recognized stepped out. But seeing Judge Doran here made no sense. The judge wasn't exactly a spring chicken, so she should have been either dead asleep or just getting up. But she wasn't. She was here, and the look on her face wasn't too kind.

"Judge, Judge Doran," Mark called as she approached.

"Where's...where's my daughter, Borden?"

Confused, Mark didn't know what to say. "I...I don't know," he said, shaking his head and shrugging his arms. He almost told her he'd just gotten there himself but didn't. That would no doubt only serve to cause additional confusion.

"Where are you coming from? Where you been?" the judge shouted at Mark. While she'd never been the picture of rainbows and lollipops, he'd never seen the elderly justice speak so curtly. Not even in her own courtroom. But there was no mistaking that something maddening had riled her up.

Mark opened his mouth to answer but only managed a few grunts and stutters. The judge, a tall, broad woman as solid as an oak tree, blew right past Mark without another word. As he had left the door open, he reckoned the lady took it he was leaving the garage rather than the house. So that's where she headed.

Mark stood and watched her go. His first instinct was to follow her and help her if he could. That was just the sorta guy he was. But he also was worried about what he'd left behind. God only knew what the other part of him had been doing.

Suddenly, he felt ashamed but worse; he wasn't even sure why.

He turned back in the direction of the house and driveway and started walking, not fast but certainly at a modest gait.

There came such a tormented cry from behind him that his heart almost stopped, and icy tendrils of fear crept up his spine. The next instant, wood cracked hard against wood as Judge Doran thundered from the garage

"The fuck did you do, you God damn retard?" the judge yelled. Mark turned to face her but stumbled back when he saw the pistol that looked too large for even her hands, pointing straight at him. Mark's hands flew up.

Behind him, another car crashed down the driveway, the motor roaring like some angry devil.

Amidst the chaos, still unsure of how he came here, Mark Borden started to panic. And being a little different than the average person, Mark also panicked a little differently. He slammed his hands against the sides of his head and tried to block out the noises assaulting him. But, unfortunately, he couldn't, so he ground the heels of his palms harder and harder into his temples.

Judge Doran was coming up behind him.

A police car approached his front.

The car slid in the gravel as the driver braked, and the tires fought to find purchase.

"Look at me, you bastard," the judge called furiously. "I said, look at me!" Then, finally, the words reached Mark. Despite his attempts, he could not block out the world around him. It was just too loud, too demanding.

Mark turned to face the judge just as bright fire barked out of the business end of the pistol she carried. There was one, then two large claps of thunder and Mark felt the rounds slam into him. He fell to his knees, then fell back to the ground. He heard shouting but couldn't make out the words.

He landed roughly on his back. There was no pain, only a cold, icy sensation that started in his chest and spread through his body. He saw the night sky above, lightening into a new day, a day he would not live to see.

There were more booms of thunder around him. Shouting and screaming.

Finally, he saw a face looking down at him. It looked sad and tormented. It was the face of Tom Harper.

"Borden, damn it, are you okay?"

Speaking had never been easy to Mark, but he found the task much more difficult now. "I was me for a while. But now he's gone," was all that Mark could say.

Harper spoke, but the words had no sound, and his face was blurry. Soon, Mark saw nothing but darkness.

TOM HARPER WAS IN A WORLD OF PAIN. HE'D LOST A LOT OF BLOOD and had been weak as water when he could finally stem the bleeding and locate a car with the keys still in the ignition. Thankfully, the round had passed through his thigh without clipping anything important. Good thing for him that Sparkman was a lousy shot.

He knew where the man they called Mr. Dark and Scary was headed, and he knew the man was on a mission.

Things with the sheriff didn't add up. But even though he knew Sparkman had married Judge Doran's daughter, he had never considered either Beatrice or the judge to be in on it.

When he watched as Doran gunned down the poor Mark Borden before he could get stopped and order her to stop, he wasn't sure which one fell on the side of righteousness, but he was pretty sure that even here in Winchester County, gunning down an unarmed person was still a crime. When Doran had also aimed her weapon at him, Harper had only the thinnest of moments to react. He did so by dropping the judge where she stood.

Now, the last one standing, he checked on the two. He watched as the life left Mark Borden. He felt terrible about that. After all, he'd brought the man in. Delivered him right into the waiting arms of Sheriff Sparkman, it seemed. It mattered little he didn't know what he was doing. The fact of the matter was, he should've.

He moved over to the judge.

She was once a handsome, if not beautiful, woman until drink and age had stolen most of her looks. Now, lying prone on the ground, the gun having fallen eternally out of her reach, she looked much older than he'd ever seen her. Pale blue eyes stared toward heaven.

He bent low, checked for a pulse and found none. He slowly stood up. His head was swimming, and he almost lost his balance but caught himself before taking a spill. He slowly trudged to the open garage door and held firm to the doorframe. He sucked in air and waited for his balance and vision to return. Slowly, they did, somewhat but not entirely. Stepping in, he flipped a switch, and suddenly the interior was awash in yellow light.

What he saw in that glaring light took his breath away and almost brought the seasoned law enforcement officer to his knees.

It was Beatrice Sparkman. It didn't take a medical examiner to know that. But she was in bad shape. Tom moved closer to her. He still held tight to his service revolver but didn't think it would be needed. Her body looked worse than any roadkill he'd ever come across. And after all these years on the highway, he'd seen more than his fair share of mangled bodies. Nothing could compare to this.

When he noticed the freezers, their lids still wide open, frozen mist rising into the air, he hobbled over to them, looked in, turned, and vomited. Tears welled in his eyes. He began weeping. His body shook and trembled. Harper had to use the side of the freezer to keep him upright.

"Jesus Christ," he muttered.

After a while, he composed himself.

He needed to call this into the state police. He had to tell someone what had happened here and what had been going on for quite a while by the looks of the dead children.

The news would rip the town apart. Of that, he had no doubt. But this was Farmington. This was Winchester County, and the whole place had been ripped apart and would undoubtedly be so again.

Outside, the first rays of the sun were slipping from beneath the horizon, and the world was cast in a grey tint. The car he'd commandeered looked a hundred miles away. His state-issued cruiser was closer, and he decided he'd instead reclaim it than make the farther walk to the deputy's car.

Harper took careful, measured steps in that direction. He was careful and cautious not only for his benefit but with the sheriff dead. Who knew how long it would take for someone to think about checking on his property?

A twig snapped off to Tom's left, and he twirled faster than he thought possible, bringing his sidearm up to bear. He stopped himself from squeezing the trigger at the last possible moment.

A little girl stepped out from a copse of trees two dozen feet away. Dressed like those poor little ones inside the freezers, this child was very much alive. She looked terrified and half-starved.

"It's okay," Tom said, though he couldn't shout. "I'm with the highway patrol. Everything's okay now." The girl hesitated at his words as if they were too good to be true. Then, as Tom watched, another girl emerged. And then another.

They slowly started stepping his way. Tom put away his gun and met them halfway. The first girl, she said her name was Kathryn, was the only one that would talk at first. He helped them into the car and told them he would take them into town and notify their parents they'd been found.

Again, Tom Harper was disappointed in himself. He'd heard of the missing girls. The toll had risen to eight, but he had never even considered they would be in his jurisdiction. It just seemed impossible. But he, of all people, should never presume to know what was possible and what was not. At least not anymore.

After making sure the girls were secure, he started the car, revved the engine and made a wide turn in the side yard before heading down the driveway for the road. At the end of the drive, he checked on the girls in the rearview mirror. They looked like they'd just returned from war, all shell-shocked and mum mouthed. But they were alive, and for that, he was thankful.

Here in Winchester County, things didn't always turn out so well. So, Tom Harper, shot in the leg and in immense pain, couldn't help but grin as he turned his car in the direction of town. The sun was shining just above the horizon in the east, announcing another beautiful spring morning.

ABOUT THE EDITOR / PUBLISHER

Dawn Shea is an author and half of the publishing team over at D&T Publishing. She lives with her family in Mississippi. Always an avid horror lover, she has moved forward with her dreams of writing and publishing those things she loves so much.

D&T Previously published material:
    ABC's of Terror
    After the Kool-Aid is Gone

Follow her author page on Amazon for all publications she is featured in.
    Follow D&T Publishing at the following locations:
    Website
    Facebook: Page / Group
    Or email us here: dandtpublishing20@gmail.com

R.K. LATCH

R.K. Latch is a southern gentleman with a keyboard and a wild imagination. He's an independent writer of novels, novellas, and short stories. Most of his fiction centers around the fictional southern Winchester County, Mississippi. R.K. lives back in the woods with his wife and daughter.

Mr. Dark & Scary by R.K. Latch

Edited by Patrick C. Harrison III

Cover art by Ash Ericmore

Formatting by J.Z. Foster

Mr. Dark & Scary by R.K. Latch